ALSO BY JANET KAUFFMAN

Places in the World a Woman Could Walk

This is a Borzoi Book
published in New York
by Alfred A. Knopf

Janet Kauffman

Collaborators

A NOVEL

ALFRED A. KNOPF · NEW YORK · 1986

THIS IS A BORZOI BOOK
PUBLISHED BY ALFRED A. KNOPF, INC.

Copyright © 1986 by Janet Kauffman
Published in the United States by Alfred A. Knopf, Inc., New York,
and simultaneously in Canada by Random House of Canada Limited, Toronto.
Distributed by Random House, Inc., New York.

Library of Congress Cataloging-in-Publication Data
Kauffman, Janet.
Collaborators.
I. Title.
PS3561.A82C6   1986   813'.54   85-45595
ISBN 0-394-55080-3

Manufactured in the United States of America
First Edition

For
Jerome McGann, Maureen O'Reilly, Nancy Steele,
and, of course, always,
for
Nicholas and Matthew Borland

One

1 My mother lied to me about everything. She told me she believed in Hell. She told me she was a pacifist, a good Mennonite, and could never kill, not even in self-defense. She crooned and ranted and cooked up powerful storms of lies that held like uncalled-for weather over my childhood. I wasn't surprised when satellite pictures of Earth showed global swirls of cloud, an enormous confluence of currents—I recognized it, that bauble, the one blue marble she called her Beauty. Why wouldn't a child believe her? She was no fake; she said riddles were doll-baby mathematics.

She told me she taught herself to swim, at a bend in the St. Joseph's Creek, and I believed it. She said that she learned to touch at the muddy bank, go under, and return stroking, fifteen feet one way, fifteen feet back, until her turns were as smooth and sure as the right and left breathing. On the sly she told me, and more than once, that the world had nothing to do with God.

2 At Rehoboth Beach, my mother digs her heels in the sand, faces the ocean, and, on her own cue, collapses on her back beside me.

Are you all right? I ask.

Sure, Dovie. Don't worry.

Water collects in the shadows beneath her knees. Every time she breathes, another rush of water pools there. I'm small enough to lie beside her and use her shade. There, I am invisible; I am in hiding, in the only darkness she offers me. But if I raise my head and look over my chin into the daylight, I can see the blond unshaven hair on her calves, glitters of sand among the hairs, and, beyond her legs, clear strips of navy-blue ocean and white sky. The things I see have, as frame, one of my mother's limbs; that's how she places herself, convenient, dismembered, for such compositions. She doesn't realize that her body is breakable, but for me each glimpse of her, whole, is a resurrection. I believe it is she, not I, who attaches her body this closely at the edge of everything. When I look up, there is an arm, a leg: she points, or kicks, or lays claim, in my view, to all that she can.

It is early August. We lie in slopes in the dune—loungechair slopes we have carved out by hand. Nearer the water, a few sunbathers stretch out their arms and legs on striped towels; and along the wet shore close to the waves, two babies crouch like penguins and work at towers in the sand. Nobody bothers my mother.

I happen to be beside her—I happen to be her child, and she acknowledges this, sometimes rubbing my back with the oiled palms of her hands. She cups my shoulders and slides her palms down my arms. All the same, I'm a ghost to her. Lightweight. I hover, physically apparent since birth, but not yet fully attached to the world, not weighted with the bodily form she approves: working thighs, an emphatic pelvis.

I am not aware of my bones—and I know this now, as I may have known it then, when she hugged me routinely and I hugged back, holding her ribs or sometimes the bones of her arms. The memory of embrace is the memory of breakneck collision. I am feeble, and my mother is knuckled and ankled like other Mennonite women, constructed to break ground, to dig. She bends over and around me, with the interior light, gray and green, of her approach, and the salt air from under her arms—a tent settling over center poles when forest light, daylight, is shut out. She brings the artificial light of her own bones and skin. I live like a camper, off the roads, homeless by somebody's choice. My face is scrubbed. I am unemployed, and nobody's lackey. Except hers. Whatever she knows about digging—digging to China, grave digging—I am too thin and too timid to comprehend. It is my own mistake that I recognize my arms and belly as skin, as flesh, while she shakes my shoulders with her hands and says, Oh, my baby. Her thumbs can press against any bones they choose.

But my mother's shoulders are fleshed and rounded, the firm shoulders of a swimmer; and, for this, she is a scandal at family reunions when my Mennonite cousins and aunts sit on the edge of the pool at the Bucks County Park, their prayer caps tucked under strapped white rubber swim caps. With her feet in the water, my mother takes the shape of a hometown mermaid, a renegade one—no dreamer—with short blond hair.

My mother is not a beauty, but what child knows? She has teeth I take care to watch when she laughs—an open-mouthed rattled laugh that comes from the back of her throat. Her teeth snare that laugh and wrap it up like a gift, struggle it after a minute into a manageable smile. What softness she has is detachable—there is the softness of her hair, thick, dirt-blond, full of air; and the softness of her shoulders. She does nothing in the usual way to beautify herself, no lipstick or rouge, although she uses her eyes and turns of her head to draw attention away from her harshness. There is a ranging boniness to her face: she is jaw and nose and skull. But her face is tamed by her will, by discreet internal commands. She tries to be careful. She doesn't want me to think *animal* or *skull* or *creature* when I look at her. But I am her daughter, and that's what I think.

My mother cannot take her eyes away from the water. She stares straight out, past the breakers, to the dark line where the ocean diminishes, where it loses us. She talks to me, but I'm invisible, a fleck of her thinking. My nub of a brain works, works, and pitches across the summer air that separates us. She's ahead of me most of the time, and she's tricky. Her eyes take on the dim blue or gray of the day's sky—whatever the day—reflective of light, unrevealing.

My mother is not the distinctly drawn mother of magazines; she is not clear-cut.

If all of my loved ones were drowning, she says to me—to the me that is no one—and I had the strength to save one, I'd save Ruth.

You could save two, I say. But I know I am going under.

I said if I could save *one*, my mother says. Ruth is the luckiest woman I know. She'd be saved.

Ruth owns a beach house on Cape May. She doesn't farm.

My mother says we will visit her sometime and sit on her porch or step off her back steps and walk to the lighthouse. They know each other from high school, and they write to each other—they never call; they write long typed paragraphs. News, my mother says, when she tears the envelope open.

My mother favors lucky people, and that is a clear injustice she sets down before me as my special treat.

The lucky ones live, my darling, she says. They have nothing to say about it.

Am I lucky? I ask.

You may be. You're lucky to be a girl. Men are really unlucky; they have a hard time just living. Especially the powerful ones. They don't know what to do with the world, except run it.

What does Ruth do?

Ruth? She does all kinds of things. We'll visit her sometime.

What does she do?

I told you. You name it, she does it.

Does she have a daughter?

No.

Then aren't you lucky, too?

Of course. You know I'm lucky. I'm not going to drown, is that what you're thinking?

I flounder, unrescued, wherever I try to step, like the footed farm child I am, stranger to beaches, afraid of the water that rolls and keeps rolling, pushing its last breakers like a fence towards me. The gentler lake of the sea must be somewhere out there, hedged, private. My mother is no help at all. She sends me off by myself, her fingertips cold on my shoulder— Get your feet wet.

And she watches. I walk away to the wall of the ocean as it falls. I calculate how to touch the collapsing wall, how to tag it, and how to rush off within my own splashes, up the beach ahead of the foam and onto the dark sand that is colder than the spray of the waves.

My mother has me surrounded. I must be hers. Anyway, I am her daredevil. At the edge of the ocean, I wait for a wave to move in, and when a big one rolls over on its side and comes at me, I squint my eyes and watch until the last moment for her sake, and then, like a baby sent to touch a dead body, experimentally—verification only a child, bounteous, could give with surety—in that child's wretched trembling for her own lively self, I touch the falling water with my fingers; then turn and run. Run towards my mother. Keeping ahead of the curve of foam. My toes spread apart in drier sand and I slow and slow. At her knees, I see my mother is looking beyond me, past the water. She's seeing the shells at the bottom of the sea, pearls on a murky platter.

I drop in the space beside her that is first of all cool. I sit there, curled, her shell, right at hand. But after a time, the air turns feverish. Her warmth and the sun's warmth generate spirals, whirlwinds, around me, miraculously inside of me, and I sit up straight, extending my neck for cooler air.

My mother pulls me over; her hands catch the sides of my head. She draws my whole head down into her lap, my ears against her thighs. There is darkness and a surprising breeze between her legs, and she rubs my hair with her fingers. I feel grains of sand against my cheeks. Her motions are so sudden, consequences of rapid thoughts, which she doesn't disclose— her thoughts are all silence—and I am her hand-held charm. The strands of my hair, which she wraps around her fingers, are dry and hot and foreign. My hair belongs to some other child, a parched desert child.

My mother lifts my head. She holds my face towards the water.

There's no end to it! she says, of the ocean, as if it could be said of nothing else in the world.

My throat closes in the dangerous air. I fill with worry and it aches in my throat. There is nothing I will be able to prove to her. I see a short, handwritten letter: *I am here*. It would make her unhappy.

Soon my mother will go for another swim. To prepare myself, so I will not hold my breath the whole time, I imagine in careful detail my mother swimming the ocean, each ocean, out and out, swimming past channel buoys, past the last gulls; she swims the way doves fly, steadily, tirelessly, across the Atlantic and around the horn of Africa. A dot, she flurries a blue globe, tours like a minnow into Indian, Malaysian estuaries. Among strewings of islands, she swims the Pacific, and curves with the equatorial waters, then dives to the south along the Chilean coast, colder and colder, through the sharp turn of the Straits of Magellan, and then, warming with warm Atlantic currents, northward and northward. The waters are blue, aqua, translucent. She skims, glides, too far from Florida to be seen, up the Carolina coasts, slowing for Delaware. She could go on, but I always bring her back. She strokes to shore with the unvaried rhythm I have seen her practice in calm water. She swims very close to shore. I recognize her, the upswing of her chin, the O of her mouth, the rolling shoulders. Just beyond the breakers, she lets her legs fall underwater, and she walks upright through the swells. On the beach, she brushes water down from her arms, down from her legs, and with quick shakes of her head, she spins her hair to the sides and walks to where I am in the sand, showering me.

I am warm and cold at the same time, however I think of her.

My mother lets go my head, and—there—I notice myself again, in my own outlined body, in my blue swimsuit a shade darker than hers. I push my fingers under the sand at my sides, and it covers them over, making a monster of me, fingerless, handless. I push under my feet. Imagine a child bounced on her torso along the beach, poor thing. That's me.

You watch! says my mother, I'm riding those waves. And she lifts herself from the sand in one sidelong, thoughtless motion. She is halfway down the beach. I pull out my hands and feet—I'm whole—and up on my knees, I stretch my back to watch. She hits the water's edge and she slows all her motions. Even the water splaying out from her sides falls away stunned, whole droplets separate and distinct. Her fingertips touch the water, pull through it, and more finely visible disruptions occur. Then she sweeps herself up and over an incoming swell, momentarily gone. On the other side, she turns herself quickly around. Now a floater, she's swept and swept and lifted my way. Here she comes. I wave to greet her, my arrival. She waves once, her whole arm up, then down, and she turns away. She walks out, more slowly than before, farther through several breaking waves until she is deep in the water. She waits through a series of swells, lifting with them, and then with a large roll, she rises as if she would jump, horseback, whaleback, and she stretches her arms out and catches the building wave behind the cresting, its frilled mane there for her, and she rides, weightless again, headlong home. When the wave breaks and pulls back, my mother digs in her toes and leans to the beach, then rises against the undertow, against gravity, and stands up easily. She walks out of the water, shaking her head and flapping her arms. She kicks one leg out, stamps it in sand, kicks the other leg, too, and stamps. Her mouth hangs open and she walks towards me. At my side, she uses my head like a post to turn herself around; she kisses me, dripping water on top of my dry hair and dry shoulders, and then she falls down beside me.

There! You should try that! she says. Although she can see I am simply a toy, with no power of my own for covering the distance, no will of my own for joining forces.

When can I try? I ask.

Float, first. We'll practice at home.

She might as well say to me, Dovie, fly. We'll practice when nobody's looking.

Have you tasted the salt? my mother asks. Here.

She holds out her arm to me, the twist of muscle at the top of her forearm—Taste it.

I do what my mother says. I lean over, and with my mouth, which seems small now, and with my tongue, which is like a bird's tongue, short and stiff, I lick her arm. Twice. And push my tongue back and forth through my lips, scraping my teeth, sucking back the salt. I taste something that tastes like the sea, which may be the salt, but I feel on the tip of my tongue the trace of the hairs of her arm, a print of her sea-swimming arm. And I lick my own arm, which is a lifeless arm, elastic and flattened, not my own at all, not anyone's.

I have nothing that isn't hers.

Salty, I say.

My mother sends me away, down the beach to meet my father and brother with their bucket full of black shells. I am her messenger and I run quickly to this man with the young man's face, who seems always just out of reach of my arms. I swoop by him, backtrack, and he does not catch me by the elbows or scoop me up, but bends down for a shell, blows the sand from it, and holds it out to me.

Look at this one. He holds it by the side, and I take the shell without touching his fingers.

Mother's licking the salt off her arms, I tell him.

Then we're standing beside her.

It's grainy, she explains.

You're tasting it, my father says. You're probably not feeling it.

This is how it goes. My mother leans back and straightens the shoulder of the arm she has licked; then she sticks out her whole tongue and licks again, largely.

Salt dries, she insists, I feel it. I feel the edges of crystals.

That's not table salt on your arm. He is smiling, my father is, with his puff of brown hair and large brown mustache, like a boy in costume, acting up.

The angles of crystals, my father goes on, are microscopic. It's unlikely a human tongue could appreciate them as edges.

Unlikely? My mother decides they will stop here. She looks at me: I'm her punctuation mark.

Unlikely, he says. He sees it coming, but cannot in good conscience omit the qualifier. I'd say close to impossible, he adds.

Close to impossible, then, my mother concludes, as she liked to conclude, with the possible in the vicinity, right at hand, but camouflaged like a wild thing the color of sand, and burrowed in.

3   You don't have to answer, my mother says. I could keep my mouth shut for days when I was your age.

She brings her teeth together and closes her lips in a line, she is that powerful. Through the Sunday songs, the grievances, outcries and accusations, the first-call prayer, she sits silent on the pew beside me, all her own. She swallows God or rolls him around in her mouth, or lets him disperse through the avenues of her brain. Whenever she likes, she swallows *yes, no;* she chews at her cheeks and hollows herself. She is severe with song and never allows words from her throat to be music only. If music is accompanied by words, she takes it as something dictated, she doesn't pretend it's not, with its questions and answers, embellishments, figures. She won't ignore the arrangements of premise, conclusion. She says never dismiss the *talk* of the tune. Every singsong she treats as a crowd of words, and she is vigilant, gulping, ready for trouble. Words, infiltrators, transport a human weaponry—machetes, bombs, cyanide, firecrackers bound to go off—it is like that.

My mother closes her mouth—knife-swallower, sword-swallower, fire-eater, bitterest-pill swallower.

You don't have to say a thing.

Song volleys from ceiling to wall to wall, an elaborate effect for a plain room of a church, new-painted white every summer and as clear any month as the sworn mind, a hospital hosed.

Front and back, women on our side sing the questions, and across the corridor of the aisle, men with their chests proffered

up like boxes give the answers. Nobody looks at the hymn-
books; the words are in us and out of us, marked with a savory
breathing, claimed and kissed like wounds as they touch the
tongue:

> What can wash away my sins?
> Nothing but the blood of Jesus.
> What can make me whole again?
> Nothing but the blood of Jesus.

If you say so much as *boo*, my mother says, you get one
hundred percent. But zero is magic. Zero's the number of
God.

4 You see by the postcards, it was the time of my
life, she said, and she showed me three cards, from three men,
one of a flat lake with rowboat and fisherman; one of the same
lake uninhabited at dusk; a third of a painted silver lake with
cartoon catfish clowning around a hook and a beckoning worm.
The messages were identical: Dear one, etc., etc.

This was the grandfather, this the son, and this *his* son.
She shuffled the cards.

They were always of the same mind, she said.

My mother liked to talk to me then through the long
evenings we worked together in the stripping room of the
tobacco shed, a dry basement room, aromatic and overheated,
where we pulled the cured tobacco leaves from the stalks and
sorted and sized them. As she talked, she wrote her favorite

words in the dust of the sizing tables, and it was my job to rub out the old words and make room for more. In boxes under the sizing tables, my mother stored her postcards, her letters from Ruth, and other important papers. Whenever we finished enough leaves for a bale, my mother would fill the press and put the wooden weight in place on top, and then she would lift me up, set me on the wooden plank for the slow ride down as she cranked the handle, compressing the bale into solid shape. The more she cranked, the lower I settled in the press. The bale firmed underneath me.

You're traveling, Dovie, she said. The world's just flying by.

When the bale was completely pressed and we'd tied it with ropes, we took a break, and that's when my mother pulled out her papers from under the tables. She showed me postcards, many sets of three, and she talked to me then about these three men and about the activity of life she called love, whose dire expression was sex. She was not very bookish about it, but dramatic in a noisy, believable way. Sex, she said, is wholehearted as swimming. A lover moves like deep water across the beloved, like the variable waters of the ocean, unfathomable, sucking, full of collapses. The body in love, in its midst of lovemaking, returns to the individual cells, frantic blind nuclei. A reduction to one—one—one again, was quite possible, my mother said. Forget you are two-footed and unsteady, forget you have lost the streaming hair off your back.

She wrote *forget* in the dust of the table. She wrote *hair*.

My mother talked to herself, and to me, in randomly detailed rising and falling imperatives. Forget the houses you have seen, the appliances you plug into sockets on the wall. Forget walls. It's that easy, she told me, to take a naked man in your arms. This of the body is jade, she said; this, Sahara;

this, Argentinean savanna. And here, this, even this, the motionless under-ice Arctic drift. You will study geography in the eighth grade, she told me, and remember it is the body you study. The economies of the world, you will see it, are wonderful economies of flesh and wish. Earth, the beauty, is all desire. Well, you will kiss it, Dovie—and she meant, I knew it, the face of the Earth—and you will know what I mean, she said.

The child in me then that crouched down or rocketed, small and jubilant, the part of me that assumed an indistinct shape in my mother's mind—that child was the daughter she talked to about her lovers, her three lovers, grandfather, father, and son, whom she loved equally, she insisted on that, and dreamed of equally; whom she had coupled with compassionately, each in his sickness, and each in his rigorous self. I asked her which was my father, and she said that the man who took us in the summer to the ocean, who walked on the beach with my brother, that was my father. He was the one we saw in the house every day, the one we called father, the one who told stories at night I could never remember, who gave me presents that disappeared, who embraced me like air. She did not describe her love for my father, although they had lived in a house with a wide porch for many years, and had their two children, and lived through at least one terrible time together, the time she didn't mention until I told her one Saturday morning when I was twelve that I was bleeding, and then she sat down in the middle of the floor and told me what she could tell. My father was not part of that story, either, but he must have known it; and he must have helped her to sleep, and made love to her quietly when I was conceived. He is the one between all the lines, the one who walks in and out of the house, comprehending.

But the grandfather, the father, and son, as she told it, she loved in order—grandfather first, then the others, and for one summer, all together.

I'll tell you, Dovie, she said, when the sun was shining and when it was not. I won't just add it in.

She wanted me to believe that. And she did give accounts of a number of rainy days. But the first story I heard was heated with a lavish, earthward-flowing light that I've looked for ever since, as if it would grant me, as it seemed to grant her, the blessedness of the simple truth, unexaggerated and unencumbered.

The grandfather, she said, was eighty-three at the time she met him, a Monday noon, outside the Blue Ball branch of the National Bank. After the museum chill of the bank, they stood on the sidewalk, the sun on both shoulders, both pairs of shoulders, and they set their heads back until the top vertebrae of their necks gave out small cracks. They adjusted their faces in the same way, at the same angle, to catch the brunt of the sun on their foreheads. The warmth spread around the sides of their eyes.

They nodded, then, to each other, the way people do after understood toasts with wine, a nod apiece. He said, very fancifully, You look like a farmer's daughter.

I know tobacco, she said.

Don't we all, he said. The greenest thing that grows is tobacco.

The two of them sat on the concrete base of the Blue Ball clock. He wore a straw hat and his eyes were full and elongated, the brown of the irises strewn with gold flecks like the scarab leaves of partially cured tobacco.

We are paid well for growing a noxious plant, he said, with what she decided was glee. She saw two gold teeth.

Each reached for the other's hand, and in this case the ordeal of love began that simply. They walked to the bus stop and took the Blue Ball bus to the end of his gravel lane.

It all happened before I was born.

I wasn't thinking of children, my mother told me. I was thinking: this is a man who does not approve torture, who does not understand.

She talked as if that were some kind of marvel, her discovery at last of goodness, amazement, within the mind of a man.

5

The world is political and chromosomal, she says. It's flux and biological drive. Everything in the world, she says, is natural. Except for a few innovations. Such as *dominion*, as she calls it, God's or anyone's. Marketeers, spoilers, grabbers, blasters, mashers, hounds, the whole hoopla—*that*, she says, is what the idea of God has made of decent men. Oh, my baby, she says, what you don't know.

She hands me a pair of binoculars and we walk on the path around the barn, in late April, out between the tobacco fields, newly plowed and harrowed, pale on the surface with chalky bits of limestone that set a twist of bitterness in the air. The taste infiltrates and catches, sharp, just at the edge of the tongue.

With every other step, she squeaks her resined birdcall, a narrow red cylinder hung around her neck, and she says whatever she wants to say, without looking at me. She knows I'm there; but she isn't sure what's coming in from the south, towards the trees. She notes the clouds; she looks between them.

As soon as we reach the shadow of the woods, she stops her talk. She interrupts herself and lets any subject slide.

We enter the woods with careful steps, through the first wall of dark green light, and inside, in full shade, we stand with our heads thrown back, contorted, and the skin of my mother's neck arches a pearly, underwater white.

She scans the next wall, the penitentiary's, flat at the end of the woods, perpendicular rocks, and through the shadowy falls of the rocks, and the wash of trees, and up, and back— my mother's neck twists, mother-of-pearl. Finally, directly over her head, the sky opens up, an intermittent, breathable surface, out of the reach of the locust trees.

With the heavy black binoculars pressing circles around our eyes, we search the tops of the trees for warblers. Glass upon glass, the lenses bring them in, birds so small, fleeting, at such a distance, their presence seems more like thought, or wish—brief and colorful motions my mother will trace and decipher. She names them—palm, cerulean, black and white— and calls them back into utter simplicity.

The yellow rump, look, that's the myrtle, she says. Sweet pie, the place is loaded!

6   It wasn't Macedonia. I know it wasn't. But it was rolling, difficult land, and there were purple and pastel flowering gardens, and the orchards were bordered with hedgerows

of black raspberry and currant. On the slopes, fields were contoured in small sections, which shifted each summer through strips of color—aquamarine of oats, the variegated green and yellow of wheat, and the coarse, dark velvet green of tobacco.

All this was more than pretty; but daily life was no idyll, my mother warned me. She liked to warn me. People weren't blind. The penitentiary was not quite out of sight. People didn't deny it. My mother didn't deny it. Outside the prison walls, too, especially there, my mother pointed to disorder— Crush bottles by the side of the road; a stranger thrown from a motorcycle near the springhouse; random storms that brought down elms.

But people embraced these things. They took up collections. If there was disaster anywhere in the world, somebody chartered a plane for Mennonite Relief, and my mother and busloads of others packed up, flew to Honduras or the Philippines, to rebuild a wooden school that had blown to sea. When she came back, my mother showed me her callused hands and spread the palms up—See, empty-handed, she said. She made it a point not to buy souvenirs. We don't tan, either, she said, and touched her arm to mine, to match them.

Nobody went to war. There were no wars.

In Mennonite Bible school, an easy assignment was to draw a "good man." My mother said I won a blue star, and it wasn't because the crayon man on my paper held twenty children with crutches in the crooks of his arms. She said the man looked naturally, undeniably good. His circular eyes ignored the halo over his head, a gold-crayon halo as thick and wide as an inner tube. Also, he wore a long robe, like a girl's.

Goodness has nothing to do with convention, my mother said. It has nothing to do with sentiment.

She made distinctions.

Goodness was passion—an ongoing, cumulative passion, a hoard of energies and decencies stockpiled against the day evil, that armored slug, turned up in the garden. And evil, of course, was not sin. Sin was what human beings *did*, when they acted most freely according to nature.

Evil was something else; it violated nature. It was loathsome, pestilential, chaotic. It showed itself always as violence—an explosive. Under its own power, it crawled into the garden, with some kind of time-release mechanism preset and clicking. Everyone knew it. You walked outside in the morning with a cup of coffee to pick some tarragon leaves or fennel, and—*bam!* That was that.

People knew it could happen. They were wary.

Even so, everybody enjoyed the scenery. They leaned back against the boards of the barn, in the afternoon just before supper, and rubbed the velvet tobacco leaves in their palms, and rubbed until in the dark between their hands they held gummed, scented globes, and their palms were crusted with tar.

Tobacco kept people healthy. Nobody thought to smoke. The plants were as tall as women, lithe ones, the stalks almost woody. Between Labor Day and frost, it was harvest, and men in overalls and women in dresses bent with long-handled shears, cutting tobacco; and Marlene Beecher and Johnny Smoke, from town, volunteered to spear; and tourists from other places came in cars to watch our family walk down the rows, one after another, and to watch the tobacco plants lean to the side and fall like small timber.

In the cleared spaces between the rows, where the dust was red and soft as face powder, my brother and I played with the huge fallen leaves. My mother said we played there, and I have a few of my own memories, too. We shredded the leaf away from the center rib, and then smashed the rib with a gray rock. With the tobacco juice from the veins, we stirred up thick red pies in the dirt.

In this field, when I was eight, my Aunt Sarah called out: Andrea Doria, you drive.

That's all it took. I tossed away the tobacco leaf and crossed the field to the gray tractor, where my mother showed me the left-foot clutch, the right-foot brake, three gears, the throttle. From then on, I drove the tractor that pulled the tobacco wagon—a scaffold wagon, where my mother and father hung up the stalks that my grandfather and Aunt Sarah, Marlene and Johnny Smoke, and the work crew from the prison had already speared onto long wooden laths. The first couple of years, I stood up to brake on the hills, to give my legs weight.

It's true that my name is Andrea Doria. There it is. My mother took to the name of a sinking ship. She said she liked the sound of it, that's all. I tried to believe her. She always paid attention to the news, but she claimed, in this case, she didn't make the connection.

For me, what was most remarkable about my name was its worldliness—it wasn't biblical. I wasn't Esther or Miriam, and that was enough.

Anyway, a name is nothing, my mother ended up saying. I don't know what the fuss is. What about Lars Skryzinski? What does it matter? You get to know him, the name disappears, she said. But Lars doesn't know *us*, does he, Dovie?

Why don't you say my name, then? I asked her.

It's a special name, she whispered. I always say it to myself. But let's talk about Lars, she said, veering. He's a dreamboat, don't you think?

That summer, Lars Skryzinski was writing his book on manual labor. It was published, *Affectional Handwork*, and his findings are well known now. Some people got out of farming as a result; some came to it.

He slept in our house for a few weeks in August, on the daybed. He was already an old man, narrow-chested, with long white hairs on the sides of his head. Every day of the week, he wore identical unpressed khaki shirts; and with his recorder, notebook, and pens on chains hanging from both shirt pockets, he looked mechanical, a kind of contraption. He walked in the fields, talking into his machine. In the barn he asked his questions, held out the microphone, and said, Yak, just yak.

He'd already finished his studies of various trades: lumberers, road crews, pearl divers. Farmwork was last on his list, and my mother said anybody could see he got carried away. He saw one thing but not another, like a lover. Since it was the summer and the leaves intervened, he didn't see the prison. He looked around, with his riveted, pinched eyes, but my mother believed he didn't quiz her enough. There was no way to tell him what he missed, she said. She'd written him a few letters, after he'd gone, to fill him in, but she thought that without her voice coming off his tapes, he couldn't pick up on her thought. He fell for tobacco, like anybody else, she said. It was only natural.

In his book, Skryzinski wrote, "A prophet could not have dreamed up a more alluring crop for the pious" than tobacco, a semitropical weed, exotic, gold in its curing, "a beautiful body of a plant," he wrote, "its one use, its only use, a sin."

Little does he know about *use*, my mother said at that part, not to mention sin! She loved reading the paragraphs to me. Listen to this, she said: "Crops worked by hand seduce the worker through the physical, sexual self, beyond it, to the *sensual being*. Work with cigar tobacco involves the touching of hand to plant more than seven times: planting, transplanting, topping, suckering, cutting, spearing, hanging up and taking down, and stripping the cured leaves. The work is bodily, passionate work. Tobacco pales the face." That's what he says, my mother assured me: "Tobacco pales the face. From June to September, farmers and families in this country eat less, and toss at night like adolescents."

We certainly heard *him*, didn't we! my mother said. Some people, she said, you show them a pretty place, they go dreamy, that's all. They forget everything they know. They forget every book they've ever read. She said Lars looked across a field as if it were ground that had risen up for him and floated in midair, where he could blow out his breath and kiss anything that moved. He counted up men and women in the field as if he were counting angels. I told him, you wait, she said. You wait until Labor Day and we cut. But he missed that. He missed every day in September, Dovie. He missed the work crew down from the prison. He didn't see the whirlwind we saw.

The last day of August, he packed up his yellow car and backed out the driveway, with his long arm out of the driver's window, waving. That's how somebody drives out of Heaven— lighthearted! she said.

By Labor Day, he was probably in Brazil, in another one of those places where people use knives on enormous leaves and eat the purple root of a plant and weave feathers into the fibers of hammocks.

He was nowhere near here, my mother said.

7 In the middle of the room is the noise of rattled paper, the noise of a one-page letter, or two. The papers stop in midair, hover; hush. Then they are soaring somewhere through a long silence.

My mother is not afraid of the dark, although there are some things she is afraid of.

It is the same in almost any house, she says, it's the same in a hut—a bat in the middle of the night, in a room large enough for precise reflection of sound off the walls and off the uncurtained windows. She says you need three things: something to cover your hair—a diaper, or a size 40 T-shirt—tied back tight at your neck; some towels, to throw as traps; and the cast-iron fireplace shovel, to stun. She tells me not to count on killing.

There's never a way to get in, she says, but they get in. And there's never a way out. They never get out.

In those early years of grade school, my mother said I slept well, curled like a baby, my lips busy in sleep. I sometimes dreamed in cartoon, with *The End*, in my own cursive style, across the last dream scene. I always slept through the night, through storms, through everything, and therefore my mother thought she could tell me about the bats. She knew I liked school, especially science, and she thought I would want to know.

What if they get in *my* room? I ask her.

But they don't get in your room, Dovie.

What *if?*

There's no way for them to get in.

You said there's *never* a way, I say, triumphant. But they get in.

Oh, such a daughter, she says. Such a dove.

8

The last night of every vacation at the beach, my mother builds a campfire for me.

I ask her if there is really fire like this in Hell.

She says, Sure.

Hell roars with rivers, she says. It foams with cataracts of fire. It's a golden, molten place, expanding forever, with colossal flame Niagaras. The noise is tremendous. You hear nothing there but the falling fire and the vibration of your own thoughts, the way you hear, magnified, your own voice or your own humming when you hold your ears shut with your fingers and press.

She demonstrates, humming loud with her fingers in her ears. I try it, too.

I don't think people I know will go to Hell, I shout. But her fingers still plug her ears.

After a moment, she gets up and wraps a towel around her shoulders. She walks off to find more wood. And then she is out of the firelight, just about out of sight.

9 In the morning, at a huge whetstone in the barn, my grandfather sharpens the steel spear that slips on and off each wooden lath. When the tobacco stalks are cut and withered in the field, it is his job to pick up each one, limp as a blown-over body, and spear it onto a lath. Five stalks fill the lath, and he stacks these in heaps for the wagon to haul off later. He's trained a crew from the prison, too, and all afternoon they work together, spearing one stalk after another, one row after another. He spears steadily, in his black shirt and denim overalls, in his black-and-white-striped railroad cap with the squared-off brim.

September the third, I am driving the tractor; my mother and father are loading the wagon. All of us see it at the same time—one of those weak, spiraling whirlwinds, full of tobacco dust, at the edge of the field. It moves into the field and twists down an open row, picking up speed and drawing up into itself the red dust out of footprints. The spiral expands and grows taller; it takes on a visible shape, pale as my mother's skin. It is a very pretty thing. I brake the tractor, stall, and stop to watch. I am wearing my polka-dot shirt. I stand up very straight.

The whirlwind wanders from row to row, missing the whole prison crew, and then it takes off, diagonally, towards my grandfather.

He never sees it coming. The brunt of it catches him from behind, and he throws his hands up to his eyes. He drops the lath and the spear. In the middle of the swirl, he pushes with his arms, and his wire-rimmed glasses flash, and fly off. The whirlwind holds him, dances with him, until one sharp turn when the whirlwind spins him away, with a twirl to the side as finale. In the last of that gust, my grandfather's railroad cap, like a bit of disguise, tips back at the bill, and the whirlwind takes it.

I've never seen my grandfather without his cap. Maybe nobody has, because I hear my mother say, He's bald!

My grandfather's head shines white as painted metal; it glints like chrome. In the calm, he stands surprisingly tall, with his arms against his sides. He looks less like a man than a missile, leaning to one side.

I set the brake on the tractor and jump from the seat. The prison crew watches from the next row, a line of them with their arms reaching out, ready to stop something dangerous. My mother throws down her work gloves and jumps from the plank of the wagon.

We are running, but it doesn't make any difference.

We watch my grandfather turn and tilt. He careens like a warhead—off course, out of kilter, and zeroing in on home.

10 Listen close, my mother says, these are the things you will not remember. She puts her lips close to my ear and says something like swish, swish, swish.

It is Saturday morning, and I've told her that I have started to bleed.

She says, I knew it.

I say, I'm all right. I found tampons. I know what's going on.

She says, Yes, that's right. From now on, you know what's going on. Sit down, sweet pie. Right here.

We sit on the floor of the dining room, between the table and the window, at about the same spot where, directly below in the basement, we've set up chairs for ourselves, for bad weather.

Dovie, she says, I'll tell you about the boy from the prison. There—you can see it this time of year. She points through the trees, where the outline of the stone wall cuts behind the most distant branches. If I don't focus my eyes, my mother's fingers appear to push against the prison wall, it is so small, so far away.

I say, Yes, I know. I see it.

She says, Good. Dovie, you have your own life now. You can remember and you can forget what you want.

She tells me she doesn't remember one thing before she was twelve, nothing about the town where she was born, or the first house in that town, or the second house, nothing until she moved to this county and this farm, hooked to the prison. When she married my father and added his place, between them they just about had the prison surrounded.

She takes her blue marble, her Beauty, out of her jacket pocket and rolls it across the floor to me.

Dovie, we are invisibles on this planet, she says.

When I roll the marble back, my mother picks it up, hides it in her hand, and drops it back in her pocket.

The boy from the prison, he's the one I'm talking about, she says. He *said* he was from the prison. Nobody has ever explained this to me, she says. He wore green that day and

out of nowhere, he showed up here. He claimed he broke out
of prison, but the warden said, no, nobody broke out.

Your father was working at Aunt Sarah's and it was near
dusk. Out this window, this same one, I saw the boy, coming
up to the house in his green shirt and his green pants, with
a wire cutters in his hand. He was tall and blond, all the colors
of willow, and I tell you my first impression was, a tree moving.
But he kneeled down outside this window and cut the tele-
phone cable at the wall of the house. It was easy for him. I
thought, where is my baby Dovie tucked away?

I hadn't been born yet, I remind my mother.

Yes, and thank God for that. I thought at the time, he
cannot kill an infant before my eyes. He can't do that. I thought
of the butcher knife, but I decided no, I won't. I won't do
that. I stayed where I was, in this room, until the boy walked
in the back door without knocking and came to the door of
this room and said, who else is there?

I said, Nobody.

He said, You don't say. Let's just check that out.

He took my arm at the elbow and pushed me ahead of him
through the house, upstairs, to each of the bedrooms, and
yours was full of boxes and books, and your brother's was the
spare room then.

There's nobody, I told him, but I was surprised myself at
the emptiness in each room, the boxes of air they all seemed
to be, with the walls and the glassed windows. It looked as
if no one had ever moved through the rooms or got into bed
there or shivered the first minutes against the sheets. Objects
were untouched objects: the gold chair stacked with magazines;
the chest with a comb and brush at the side; the bed with a
white bedspread thrown over it.

The boy said, So it's you and that's it?

I said, Yes, for now.

For now? So who's coming?

My husband will be here.

Nothing's cooking, he said. He sniffed the air in the hallway and steered me downstairs. Your husband can wait. I don't need a hell of a lot of time. Just get me a sack of food and a little send-off, I'm headed out.

We were in the kitchen and he was taking boxes of crackers out of the cupboard and filling a brown grocery sack. He took some cheese from the refrigerator. He took a head of lettuce.

You're crazy to live this close to the prison, he said. Look who your neighbors are. And he picked up the wire cutters, a handle in each hand, and chomped the pincers together in midair.

My neighbors are fine, I told him. You're the first criminal I've run into.

And you're a liar, he said. Oh, but these are the godly ones, hereabouts, I forgot, he said.

It has nothing to do with God. I'm talking about human beings.

Well, here is a human being for you, he said. Love your fellow man.

He set the wire cutters on the counter and came towards me. He was a boy, with a boy's blunt jaw, still swinging when he talked because he wasn't used to talk. His eyes were set far apart under his brows; they were shaded there, and he looked out from somewhere not far inside.

I said, You're just a boy.

And you're a girl, I see that, dummy.

He lifted my skirt and flipped it over my head. I said through the cloth, I have my period. You'll be a mess.

You're lying, he said.

I don't lie. I just thought you'd want to know. Some men don't like it.

When I talked, I could feel the words blow around my face, the air of them, under the cloth of the skirt.

You know so much, do you? he said. Well, I *don't* like it, you're right. Here, he said. We'll do this easy enough by hand.

He pushed me against the wall of the kitchen and grabbed at my arms. He pulled out his penis and rubbed my hands just where he wanted them. He did the work. When he finished, he wiped himself on my skirt and said, Lady, my pity goes to women. God has you marked for life. You're a wounded tribe.

He sounded concerned. He lit a cigarette and said it was always the same bad luck with women, monotonous, month after month, why didn't they bitch to doctors and find a cure. He lifted my skirt again, and pressed the palm of his hand against my belly and said, You think if I punched here it might help? You never know, he said, what might help.

He rubbed his palm over my skin, and stopped, below the navel, and said, Here, try this. And then he took the cigarette and pushed the tip of it into my skin where his hand had been.

I pulled my skirt down over his head and tightened it around him until we both rolled over on the floor. I saw the cigarette fly across the linoleum and land near the back door. He was tall, and slow in getting himself upright. I had time to get to the counter and pick up the wire cutters.

Give me the food! he said.

I backed off towards the sink, and he took the sack from the counter and walked out. When the screen door slammed shut, I felt the burn, and lifted my skirt and washed the circle with water and held an ice cube there until your father got home.

He got what he wanted, my mother says. She rolls the blue marble around on the floor.

Were you lying? I ask her.

He was just a boy, she says. But, Dovie, you're a woman now, it's the truth. That boy has nothing to do with it. God has nothing to do with it. I tell you these things, she says, because I want you to know what's what.

11

No, I haven't been born again, my mother says to a minister at the screen door, who smiles at her and leans a little off balance so that the stripes of his jacket run oblique.

I am sorry you needed something so drastic for yourself, she says.

But I've heard my mother's stories—who she'd have been and when she'd have lived, had there been a scheme for corporate deals. That is her phrase for the notion of reincarnation, rejuvenation, or any rebirthing. Anyone, she says, ought to be able to come up with one or two clever corporate deals. She makes up some oddball names for herself—Daphne, Arctotis, Howard—and warns me that no situation, wherever, whenever, is without its doses of terror. Life doesn't improve, under any circumstances.

When you were born again, my mother asks the minister, did you change your name? She pulls me by the hand, moving me onto the porch, onto the scene.

The change is inside, the man says. Read these papers.

The inside means nothing to me, my mother says. She will not take his papers.

And what's *your* name? the man asks me.

Andrea Doria.

It's a beautiful name, my mother says. She tells the man to sit on a chair on the porch, and she sits down, too. I stand beside her chair, and she holds my hand in hers. For a while, she listens to the man politely, but then she forgets and is back to badgering him.

Is that car the car of your new life? What did you trade in? That's a Lincoln, isn't it? That's a poodle inside there, isn't it? *My* name, in a previous life, was Lana, she lies. Lana the nomad wouldn't put up with this business.

I'm sorry to have upset you, the minister says. He stands.

Forget it, my mother says. She eases off. Dovie should hear such things, she says. You confirm suspicions. You do a good deed.

12 One night, in the falling snow, which is already deepening on the steps of the porch, my mother shovels a path to the lower barn, to the door of the tobacco stripping room, and I follow behind her, with my arms out on each side, my mittens dragging through the snow on the tops of the trench she has dug. My mother is just ahead of me, but blurred in the snow thrown off the shovel, and blurred again in the snow blowing down.

At the door, my mother shovels an entranceway, right and left, and the snow goes wild. She disappears one moment and then takes vague shape again, although parts of her continue swirling and she has no more definition than shrubbery or the shadow of shrubbery. But she is herself in her stirring of snow, I don't doubt it. I stand very firm in my boots, in spite of her disappearance, and wait for her shoulder to push against the door, for her arm to reach around to the light— I know I will see the arm clearly—and then we will both fall inside the room, where the snow will stop and the wet clots on my boots will slip onto the floor and go dark and be done with.

That's how it happens. Inside, my mother starts a fire in the wood burner and as soon as the heat begins to lift through the room, the tobacco flavor of the air turns dry and sweet. The damp of the foundation stones evaporates, gray to gray, lighter and lighter, and on the sizing tables the dust shifts with the changed air and settles, leveled, everywhere in a gold-brown film, with the sheen of fine talc.

We load the tables with stalks of cured tobacco and begin stripping off the leaves. It's what you would think, Dovie, she says. Her voice takes on the lavish, abrupt tone of someone explaining codes.

Of course it's what you would think. You love the father, Dovie, you love the son, and the son's son, one for the other, for the sake of the other, because if the one is loved for his goodness, so is the other, and his son, and so on as long as each claims the other, and nods. That's the connection to maintain—acknowledgment, Dovie, one of the other. I tell you this, Dovie. You are a daughter. Biology, more than society, loves lineage, inheritance. Father and son, and the next son, you find you can love one, and Dovie, then, after that, one is as sure as the next. One like the other presses his palm to yours, and opens the space between his lips until the cavernous zero of love says *whole*, says *there you are*.

She draws an O in the dust of the table, and I erase it.

You make a match, each time, she says, out of nothingness, a territory dark and light and shadowless, with so few entrances and exits, the kiss is both opening and closing; and lovemaking, Dovie, guarantees nothing historical, not one thing to see in the future or to hold in your hand as a souvenir. The kiss says, *now*, and the penetration, each time, *now tell me nothing*.

Her voice becomes the saying of words, the words speaking as if they could speak for themselves, as if things in the room— twine, the split wood, a jar of nails—could make sense of sounds, any utterance. Then she is silent. She takes a handful of leaves and fits them, by length, in the sizing box. The box fills quickly and my mother lifts out the longest leaves, such long ones, and ties them together at the top, a bundle the size of a child, with the leaves fanning out like a long dress. Lifting the sheaf of leaves with both hands, smoothing it, my mother puts it into the press.

I wonder who else would believe what my mother says. It is probably not love that lets me believe her. How can I love my mother? It would be as extravagant, as foolhardy, as in winter saying I love the summer, a monumental season that my memory can't even gather back. My mother's words envelop her, take her away; they make her voluminous. Which words can I claim?

But it doesn't matter; she doesn't expect a reply. She doesn't wait for sounds puffing out of my mouth. While she gives me a ride on the tobacco press, she breathes in the air and exhales it, and the words continue.

The father's father, the old one, she says, made love like the end of the world. He wandered handily over the edge, gentle as could be. He had touched his own arms long enough and pushed his fingers through the fine hairs of his head, long enough, to admit that touch is the action of forces not human; and to say that love is as creaturely as we get, unsociable, far from the blueprints, as far from glassware and coffee tables as we will travel.

The father, though, he was another one, much too hard on himself, and fixed in his thinking about who's who. The man, after all, was still working and getting himself awake in the morning and dressing and fitting his arm in his shirt. He liked to make love and go to sleep, to wear himself out, so that when it was daylight, he'd look at trees and shake his head, he couldn't believe them.

And the son, too, Dovie, it is no surprise, the son was forgetful, nothing would fix in his mind but his hunger, his thirst. He used his tongue recklessly, and his eyes; he was always hoping to glimpse a feast, like a person opening a door who is sure a long table with bowls of fruits and plates of iced desserts will stretch out, directly ahead. He thought he was starved; he thought that the world was a banquet hall, locked up, stupidly, as a trick, so that he had to scheme and break in to feed himself. But kisses, well, what could he struggle with there? He finally let himself breathe, and his eyes, with the bits of gold like his father's and grandfather's eyes, could close in the dark, too.

Dovie, with one, or the other, or the other, you touch, that's all I can tell you. You take off your shirt and lie down, or you walk to the middle of the room and touch there, each time as if God had finally admitted, I can't think of anything else.

13 My mother carries one suitcase to Honduras, a brown boxy rectangle that snaps shut with two latches. The shell of the suitcase is plastic, poured and shaped in Taiwan in a mold with a pitted interior so that the suitcase, unpressed and glued to its framework and cloth lining, presents a skin to the world that is nubbed and coarse as a toad.

On the inside of the lid, in a cloth pocket, she packs her swimsuits, both of them. She packs a red towel and a summer dress, the yellow one patterned with darker yellow comma twists. On the left side of the suitcase she arranges three pairs of brown cotton work gloves; wool socks and work shoes; cotton underwear; a box of Tampax; a gauze prayer cap and bobby pins. On the right side are the long, dark work dresses, which have no buttons, no zippers.

Mennonites lace themselves together, my mother tells tourists, who sometimes walk in the field to ask. We're held together with hooks and eyes, she says.

Mennonite Relief charters the back-lot sort of airplane, with the name of the charter service hand-painted on the fuselage, brushed on, and a thin coat at that. On the runway at the airport, the plane stirs up in the mind words like *conveyance* or *last ditch*. But my mother is the one who says to me, Take care.

A reporter wants a picture before they leave, and what he snaps is an arrangement on the steps at the plane's door of Mennonite men in white-collared shirts, and the women in dark dresses, with their hair pulled back, everybody's ears sticking out like shells, and the sun on their foreheads, flash, flash, flash. Then they step inside and the stairway is pulled away.

14   If my mother was silent all day, even if it was the middle of winter, I'd take a walk by myself, to the wall of the prison where I knew nothing but scrubland stretched away on the other side, and there I leaned against the wall or sat on the ground and propped my back against the stones, a solid continuous sofa, and I sang the whole song, over and over, the questions and the answers:

> What can wash away my sins?
> Nothing but the blood of Jesus.
> What can make me whole again?
> Nothing but the blood of Jesus.
> Oh, precious is the flow
> That makes me white as snow;
> No other fount I know,
> Nothing but the blood of Jesus.

I sang until Jesus, bloodless, evaporated; and *blood* was the word I kept for myself, the word I held in my mouth and showered in. I sang until my mind flowed with blood, and blood pooled into lakes; and blood and rivers of blood, oceans— magnificent as the fires of Hell—were the only waters anywhere in the world.

15

Collaboration, subterfuge. That is a decent living, my mother claims. Mingle, subvert. Float, dive. She juggles her favorite words. She writes them in dust on the table. Now erase those, she says.

See, she says, Madame Justice, a word in each hand; one, then the other. She seesaws around the stripping room, bending herself one way, and back.

Nobody deserves to win, don't fool yourself, Dovie.

16

Marlene Beecher, with her wide white face and her red frizzled hair pulled back under a scarf, could easily pass for a Mennonite when she helps out in the fields. But she wears purple slacks and a green halter top, and that settles that. She's one of my grade-school teachers, and she works alongside Johnny Smoke, a guard from the prison—they're volunteers. Spearing tobacco, Johnny Smoke bends like a dancer, one leg kicked out for balance. His hair's a calamitous white, and airy, so airy it lifts and floats when he moves his head, like slow-motion hair underwater. But his eyebrows are solid black lines and his skin is charry.

When Marlene and Johnny Smoke finish spearing a row of tobacco, the two of them sit in the shade of the locust woods, drinking the Kool-Aid the prison has sent along in a plastic jug. Nobody else takes a break. But they stretch out, pass the jug, and look around the field at the prison crew, at the Mennonites, at my mother and me, with the remote, leisurely eyes of travelers who think themselves lucky to be in the landscape, before going on.

Marlene works very hard, her face reddens, and she needs the rest. But my mother admires the strength in her right arm; she comments on it several times and tells me, Look at that. You see how she swings the stalk with her whole arm. The shoulder does the work. That's what it takes. You count on the major joints because the wrist is unreliable, too much like a hinge. She's got it figured out.

Because of the halter top Marlene wears, the musculature of her arm stands out and my mother says, Dovie, you see what it takes. Her back is involved. My mother points around to the men working in the field, and she means for me to see that even though their arms and backs are covered with white or blue cotton shirts, underneath the body is at work, and you can never pretend anything else.

Any time of day, I am my mother's apprentice. Her accomplice. What would she do without me, with my fists, like antennae, picking up her thoughts? She lets me drive the tractor to the barn, with the last load of tobacco, and she rides behind me, propped against the tractor's fender. The big tire turns slowly and the deep cuts of the tread circle around and pass near the tips of her fingers. On the wagon behind us, the tobacco hangs in a wall, leaves pointing down, and a dense heated air moves out from the load. Several atmospheres, hot and chill, hover in our vicinity. My father rides on the tongue of the wagon, left foot in front of the other, and to balance himself, he holds on with one hand to the first lath of tobacco. Each time I look back to check how the load rides, I see my father take off his cap, wipe his forehead, and replace the cap where the band has left a white line.

We pass Marlene and Johnny Smoke at the edge of the field; they're packing the jug and the spears and some white handkerchiefs in a knapsack.

See me before you go, my mother calls. I want to hear about the lake.

We've seen the plans, Johnny Smoke shouts. A *big* lake! Back of the prison!

Marlene wipes her arms with a handkerchief and nods. Water where there was none! she shouts. She loosens the scarf on her head and her hair puffs out at the sides, springy with small red curls. She shakes her head like a person coming out of the water, and the hair spins side to side and fluffs out some more. See you at the house, then! she shouts.

In the dark of the barn, hanging tobacco, nobody talks. It's the last work of the day and we go through it. A bitter dust falls from the top of the barn, and another dust, much finer, rises from the tobacco leaves. I stand on the plank of the wagon and loosen each lath. I give it a little shake to straighten the leaves. Then I tip the one end upward to my mother, who stands above me, on a two-by-four set on top of the wagon's scaffold. She reaches down, lifts the lath, and, one-handed, shoves it upward again, to my father in the tier above, in the dark green of the space where he hangs the tobacco, lath by lath, to cure. We move like a circus troupe, climbing, balancing on the rails, tossing whatever we have, one to the other, a precision routine that is silent except for the rustle of leaves, somebody's coughing, and once in a while a cue, or encouragement—Hold it, Dovie; or, Okay, here we go.

Through the open slats of the barn, I can see to the house, where Marlene and Johnny Smoke wait on the porch. Johnny sits on the glider, his back very straight, and Marlene stretches out with her feet off the one end, her head in his lap.

We have unloaded half the wagon when my mother says, Look at them, Dovie.

I see Johnny pat Marlene's hair, one pat, and then he bends himself over and kisses her hair, one kiss. His white hair falls over her face.

In the space above me, my mother says, Dovie. And what do you think God sees, looking around? *None* of this, she whispers.

That's how my mother cuts things apart, outlines them, with black lines. There's not much to see, but if God isn't looking, there they are.

17   The unreason of my mother, her refusal to face facts, her bodily hauling of God in and out of the room, her coloratura talk about whim, ordinary desire, her goddess talk of the bodies of disembodied men, the power of her denials, her grace, her awkwardness—she is the genie out of the bottle. I don't know how to contain her.

18 When tobacco filled the barn, roof to floor, it was a darkened world, gone green and twisted from what we knew, a remote land there for my brother and me to explore. We dropped to our hands and knees and crawled in. Under the first row of leaves, so long they dragged on the floor, we lay flat and pushed ourselves into the interior of the barn where there was nothing but the leaves like long dresses hanging over our heads. The air settled down low, against the floor, and sometimes the air stopped, crushed where it was. We lay with our faces on the floor, rested a cheek there, and breathing sideways, pulled the air to us, gasping.

The hair of the tobacco leaves, the black gum, caught in our hair, and when we could feel the tar itself, twining the strands of our hair together and tangling, we crawled to the side of the barn and stepped backwards, out the ventilating doors. On the way to the house, we played with our gummed hair. We wadded it up, stood it on end, or pressed little strips together, like the hair of children from an undiscovered place, where hair could be decoration.

Oh, you are pretty, my mother said.

She took a cake of Lava soap and led us to the outside faucet, where she held our heads under the water and scrubbed at the tar with her fingers and then with a metal comb.

I hate to do this, she said.

The water was cold and my mother worked quickly, scraping the tar from my hair, using the soap like a scrub brush. She rubbed the Lava, full of its sandy pumice, into my scalp and down my neck, down my shoulders. The water poured away, a circle of falls, at the side of my face.

Well, my mother said, I hardly recognize you two. Where did you come from?

She flicked her arms to dry them off, and I flicked my arms, too. She tossed a towel over my head.

Sweet pie, she said to me, I bet you find tar in your hair twenty years from now.

When my mother stepped away, onto the porch, I took the metal comb and worked it through my hair again, front to back.

But she caught me. Don't worry, Dovie, my mother said. Nobody's clean. Nobody's in the clear.

19 My mother said, Take Castro and his fatigues. If you make a move, Dovie, she said, you wear the same shirt ever after, you don't change your hair, nothing. Mennonites wear what they've worn, from day one. When the moment comes, when action is finally taken, out of the hills, off the farmlands, out of the caves, and the intolerable—it has to be the intolerable—is overthrown, overturned; and the lid is kicked off the trunk in the attic, and your passions and virtues are ridden in troupes, and ridden as cleanly as saints ride the stolid arm of God, when your actions rise out of the mind and you lop stuffing from stuffing—*then* you go in crude attire right down the middle of the street. Then, *then*, dress is all feathering, it grows on you, all your own; it is not fashion, not a remnant of things stripped away, not a disguise or a costume to change with new times—and they are always coming, new times, oncoming already, scuffing and digging themselves in. No. No, there is the moment you're done with the catalogues. You wear black. Or camouflage. You don't wear a king's button; you skip the kingpin's zippers. You say, no, Mr. Salesman, and tap in code to yourself, yes, yes, now let them buy the advertising. Or with nerve you can say it right off the bat: you, Mr. Salesman, I put *you* out of business.

20

My mother said she wanted to talk to somebody who knew how to think. Ruth is a scholar, she said. I want expert opinion. Anyway, she's leaving the country.

This was after my mother heard machinery at work on the prison lake and after my mother read about Lars Skryzinski's death. The *Times* said Lars fell to his death, from a footbridge over the Arawabadi River. He was eighty-four.

We waited until the tobacco was in, after the middle of September, and then we took one day for the long drive to Cape May, round trip. Ruth was leaving for Europe the following day; my mother said we should visit to talk and to say farewell, and then leave her alone to prepare for her flight. It works out fine, she said, we won't stay.

On the drive around Wilmington, I heard my mother's account of Ruth's departure from farming. It was a simple story. The day after graduation, my mother said, Ruth got herself out. She didn't fool around. That night, I had your grandfather's car, Dovie, and I drove Ruth home—to her parents' farm, with the long lane back and the white silos. She invited me up to her room, where she already had a footlocker filled with books and her winter clothes; and while she gave me an address in Philadelphia where I could write her, she took off her prayer cap and right there, she clipped her black hair. First she cut it across in a long swipe at the base of her neck, to lop off the back. And then she worked more carefully, taking small handfuls and snipping those, then pressing even smaller twists between her fingers and clipping lightly. She threw the bits of hair on a newspaper on the floor.

She said she had already figured out how to survive without holding tobacco in her arms like an offering every September. She said she could easily survive without loving her neighbors. You go right ahead, she said to me, raising your pretty plant, the one that goes up in smoke. All work comes to naught, you say. And so you go happily about your business, loving the worst for its flaws. And I said, Yes, yes, Ruth, I believe you. I believe every word you say. And I did. I still do. I have no future, Dovie. She's exactly right. That's how it is. Ruth is the lucky one. She takes a tangle and shows the twists. She told me, when I mentioned that, that she certainly didn't plan to unravel anything, that would be foolish.

But Ruth knows what she's talking about. She says kick yourself out, for good. Get lost. Ruth says you have to; it can't be all in your head.

My mother went on. I leaned my head back against the front seat and not long after we crossed the Delaware Bridge, I fell asleep. I suppose my mother continued talking, as her way of lullaby, because when I woke in the middle of the morning, in a new landscape, her voice was still there, still moving up and down its scale, holding, and going on. And it didn't matter that everything else had changed. At the edge of the road, the ground turned to sand, a white, heaped sand that looked nothing like the red dust of our fields, and nothing like the coarse sands of Rehoboth. The trees, too, had the scrubby thinness of shore growth, hit with salt, and I knew we were near the ocean. The wind blew into the car with a dampness I could see: my mother wiped the palm of her hand across her cheek and then she flicked her fingers.

Next week, she was saying, Ruth will be in Brittany, with her Marie de France. When you go to college, Dovie, read her books. I don't want you reading just Lars's ideas. Ruth doesn't get carried away. She says her motto is: Hands off. But she'll have some thoughts on artificial lakes, don't you doubt it.

We crossed several channels, where boats rested in black mud, near enormous reeds, and my mother said that at low tide, we would walk out as far as we could, past the breakwaters, and then look back. *Then*, she said, you can see what dollhouses all the mansions are. I bet we find starfish, too, in the cracks of the rocks. You won't bring them back, will you, Dovie?

Of course not, I said.

I want you to try to talk with Ruth. She's the other side of the world, Dovie. You look around down here. Just say whatever you think of to say. It doesn't matter. She's not shy.

I will, I said.

The road on the outskirts of town was uneven, full of seams, and we rattled around in the car until I was not sure it made sense to drive this far for a conversation. I could feel the long ride home, backwards over the lumpy road, through the tide marshes, the white sand and pine trees, the Delaware Bridge;

the car might as well go in reverse the way it would fold back a whole day.

It's this way, my mother said, we're about there. She turned onto a side street and we passed large frame houses with expanses of porch and wooden railings jutting out into the yards like prows of ships. The yards were not lawns, but plots of scratchy, narrow-bladed grass, and from every front porch a concrete walk led to a sidewalk, and the sidewalks turned at right angles, everything leading to the shore. My mother pointed ahead, into a whitish mist. There, there's the ocean. At the dead end up ahead, on a raised walkway, a few people moved back and forth, their heads turned to the far side, the whiteness. It won't be crowded, my mother said. Not September. The beach'll be wide open.

With some sudden braking, my mother turned in a drive. Sitting on the steps of a white-painted porch was a tall, angular woman with very black hair, which hung loose and straight from the top of her head. She wore white shorts, a white shirt. She wore lipstick.

Ruth, Ruth! my mother called.

The woman jumped up and ran to our car. She pulled my mother from the car and pulled her into the middle of the yard, where they circled together, both of them laughing and crying as they spun around, holding each other's shoulders.

My God, I have missed you, Ruth said.

Years! said my mother.

Years, they both said, and huddled again, circled again.

Look at my Dovie!

Andrea Doria, Ruth called. Let me see you.

And then they came over to my side of the car and pulled me out, one by each hand, and took me along for another ring-around-the-rosy dance in the yard. They had all the tears you'd expect, as if not only time and distance but wars and disasters had interrupted their lives and it was only by chance that they had reconvened safely, someplace where nothing would signal danger.

You're here. Come inside and change, Ruth said. We'll pack something up and eat by the water. Andrea Doria, how I adore you! Who is it you resemble? You're pale as your mother, I can see that. But I don't know. What do you think?

We have the same arms, I said. My father thinks I'll be taller.

She certainly will be taller, my mother called from the porch. She walked inside and the door slammed.

You do have your mother's chin, Ruth told me. Yes, indeed. You must write me a letter sometime, and then I'll tell you if you've got her talk. That would be something, Andrea Doria. I've memorized her voice.

Ruth's voice dropped away, like my mother's, very secret. You tell your mother to read you whatever she writes to me, I don't care. You ought to hear her. Do you know that she tells me everything? She's no mystery to me!

We joined my mother in a large entrance hall, where a bulky chandelier hung on a chain.

It's a big house, Ruth said. Scout around and pick a room to change in. We'll be here, in the kitchen. She pointed to a door that led to a room with cupboards to the ceiling.

I changed my clothes in the first room I came to, a music room, or library. I folded my clothes on a chair and slipped on a shiny blue swimsuit. I walked around the room in my bare feet. There was a baby grand piano, with stacks of music— Bach, Schubert. Ruth's desk was filled with photocopied man-uscripts with minute, ancient lettering, and on a table at the side of the room was a microfilm reader. I flicked the switch and lit up a page: "Rejected Readings of Ms. X. Chaitivel"— a page full of notes.

My mother would say, Dovie, memorize.

35 and 36 interchanged in H—125 perdiz—162 poeit—197 namerai—198 perdrai—213p.] peint—240 en]ne

I memorized. I walked like a spy, my arms and legs long and cool as I moved through the room. I saw pages stamped Bibliothèque Nationale de Nantes; and a chairful of bilingual editions and slim critical works—Hoepffner, Bertoni. On a shelf stood a set of books, leather-bound, frayed, with gold lettering on the bindings.

Ruth found me. You must learn to read French, she said. If you do, I'll give you those books. *L'Amour et les amoureux.* You will laugh and enjoy yourself. It won't surprise you. As far as love goes, Andrea Doria, we are primitives, always primitives. You ask your mother.

She talks to me all the time, I said.

She's been foolish to stay away so long.

You could have visited *us*, I said. I said that; I felt very strong, in my bathing suit, in this room in Ruth's house.

Well. No.

Why not?

Some things are better known on the page, for instance, or out of their own place. I don't want to be in the middle. In the middle, everybody's lost. Anyway, tomorrow I'm leaving for Dol.

But you could see my mother, if you visited. You could see me.

Andrea Doria, no, that's silly. You wouldn't be yourself, if

I saw you there. You'd be somebody in a field, for God's sake. I'd lose all sight of you. Apparently Lars did. Your mother knows that. Doesn't she say so? He came to look around and then, there he was, in the middle.

But we see you here, at *your* house?

I use the furniture, Andrea Doria. I do my work here, that's all. It's not a particular place. We just meet here, that's how it seems to me.

And that's how it is, said my mother. She'd changed, too, into her red swimsuit, and she looked glossy, very smooth, as if she'd never lifted the weight of a skillet.

Show her the house later, my mother said to Ruth. Let's go see the ocean.

Then my mother moved her arms, and motion itself strengthened her, filled her face and her back with light and shadow. Her legs looked powerful, oarlike, set for the water.

We walked to the beach. I carried Ruth's big red-striped blanket. My mother carried a bag of food, and Ruth took a black Thermos of vinegar punch, the one thing from tobacco growing, she said, that could do us good today. It's hot, she said. In another hour, we'll be glad for the zing.

The beach was practically empty. Gulls hovered overhead when we sat down, but when we didn't pull out the food, they gave up and flew away. The tide was sweeping out, and the ocean slipped back, almost calm, with small waves falling on themselves and pulling away, before they made much of a sound.

Walk a little, my mother told me. I must talk with Ruth.

I headed off towards a breakwater, where I'd seen a man in a green cap, walking with a bucket and pole. As soon as I moved away from the blanket, I heard my mother's voice begin, and Ruth's voice, too, interrupting, back and forth, and up from it all floated bunches of names, rising like bodies surfacing—Marlene, Johnny Smoke, Lars Skryzinski, Foulet, Tristan, Les Quatre Dols. Their voices shot back and forth, and the names, cards being dealt, one to the other, yours and yours, another, another. Five, five, six, six, seven, seven.

Even when I was sure I could no longer hear them, I could catch the mix of their talk in the fall of the ocean, like the collapse of the sea in a shell, a frilled sprawl and then a backtracking, receding, assembling.

I reached the breakwater and sat on one of the rocks, checking the low spots for starfish. When I looked back, I could see the striped blanket, the only patch on the sand. Ruth and my mother sat with their toes pointed towards the water; sometimes they seemed to be talking to the water, bringing their arms up and making gestures in that direction. But then they would lean towards each other, their heads nearly touching, and I knew their voices had dropped and they were, as my mother predicted, after years and years, marking off two distinct points on the planet.

I stepped across the rocks of the breakwater, to the next stretch of beach, and stopped quickly so as not to collide with a man and woman walking barefoot towards the ocean. I dug my toes in the sand and stepped backwards. They didn't notice me, and I dug myself in and squatted down.

The man and the woman were very large, both of them, almost doubles of themselves, one by the other by the other by the other. The woman was dressed in a green-skirted swimsuit, the man in khaki shorts, with a leather belt. The man's flesh overflowed at the waist and his thighs shifted left to right when he walked. The woman, likewise, looked puffed, inflated, with a wide face and breasts that rode on her belly. They were thinking, I could read it, their own long monosyllable, *love, love.* They looked at the water and they walked slowly, the man with his left palm resting on the woman's buttocks, the woman with her hand reaching around his side, and moving up and down, caressing him thigh to belly to chest. From time to time they kissed, just touching the edges of their lips, and when they reached the edge of the water, they walked in as if it weren't there, or were there on their silent command, and they walked in up to their knees. There they stopped and kissed again, this time drawing their bodies together, and the man's hands slipped lower on the woman's buttocks and he pressed his fingers into the skirt of her suit. He let his hands follow the roundness, down and around.

I couldn't help it—in my head I put together a list of words, not for them, of course, but for my mother: an unrelieved hum of words, a pearly string of them, hand-picked. I wrote the words out one after the other, as if they were printed and reprinted, or scrawled by hand with pen. I wrote them out slowly in my head, tracing the arms and legs of them: *flesh, none, name, death, dove.* I shaped them simple and bony and separate. *Name, none, death, dove, flesh.* I juggled the words around and looked them over. *Dove. Dove.*

I walked to a place where the sand had been packed down damp by the tide and I wrote that one out for myself, *d-o-v-e,* and then I erased it.

The beach was empty. I couldn't see where the lovers had gone, but I spent some time tracing their twinned footprints, scuffing up the sand to blur each set. Nobody'd know they were there.

When I was finished, I walked back towards my mother, my mouth full of words. They rolled there, struck like marbles, and I knew if I could open my jaw, if the chin, which was her chin, would drop, and the sounds would gather behind my lips, from out of the funnel of my throat my mother would hear them and catch them. She'd bend over and repeat them.

She'd say, Yes, Dovie, good for you.

If I was lucky, she'd talk to Ruth, and Ruth, too, would say, Andrea Doria, yes, that's the truth, nobody dead or alive could deny it.

Two

1

How many ways it would have been possible to lose her, I am coming to understand—the variable, incomprehensible ways, the savage, the random, inevitable, definitive, just and unjust ways. She said so herself. God is a numbers player and cares nothing about justice. He never was anybody's lover.

Your mother is not herself, my father said.

I imagined a tirade. I saw her standing on the porch ranting, taken over, crazed like a desert visionary.

Your mother is not herself.

It sounded at first like a decision on her part.

2

Out of the cave of the gray car, in the schoolyard, it was my father's voice. I saw the knob of his wrist at the steering wheel, and with his words, he pulled his head inside the car. His hair disappeared, up near the roof, and he wouldn't say anything else until my brother Jonas and I stepped inside.

Jonas pulled a watch from his pocket. It just started, he said, it's not over. He shunted himself over, smaller and smaller, to the other side of the back seat; and that was one inside, and I was next.

A leg first, a shoulder, just that, but the colors and weathers of outside already began to pull themselves off, unstick. Everything sucked itself backwards, diminished—the whole May Day, all of it, all of the ruckus and flutophoning and making up with pencil and paint, the teachers' voices, the cap of the Maypole, a spindle unwound, streaming—it was already far behind.

We pulled away, across the macadam, across the slope of the school hill. When I rolled up the window, the costumed, prankish shapes, child height—cowboys, bankers, angels, prisoners, sheikhs—fell and crumpled back, hushed, emptied as jars. There were no Mennonites out there anywhere.

We'd been decked out, first through eighth grade, for the morning ceremonies, lavish, with marching orders and tables of cupcakes sprinkled with red sugar beads, and cool clouded weather, hanging low. The seventh grade, my grade, were gypsy boys and gypsy girls. Boys and girls, both, wore red cloth bandannas knotted at the back of the neck. Boys and girls, both, wore earrings.

The guidelines said: *Anything, Everything! A May Day Pageant!*

Thank me, Marlene said to me, early, stepping up the steps of the porch. I got this show on the road.

She turned me around in my polished cotton skirt, lace blouse, while she nodded and squinted. She was proud of her grade-school projects. In keeping, she said, very much in keeping. She handed me two hoop earrings, big circles hung from gold chains, fine as thread, and she clipped the earrings on my ears and batted the hoops against my neck. She held out a tube of lipstick. Here. Go on. What can your momma say?

The lipstick label read SCARLET 026. The bullet-shaped tube was gold, so smooth that on the curve of its surface my face shone back and my nose spread out. The tube was not new— the stalk had been squashed, worn lopsided, with a flattened-out ledge on the top. But it twisted smoothly in the gold casing, and I adjusted the setting to suit myself, up and down. On the porch, by guesswork, I pressed the lipstick on both lips, across one way, back the other. Candy corn, that's what it was, waxen, sweetened, an old batch.

All morning, I kept my tongue curled against my teeth. I moved my tongue from one tooth to the other, counting, and I kept at it; and sometimes I curled my fingers in my palms, dug in the fingernails, one after the other, counting fingers, too, and then I counted my toes, largest to smallest, right foot and left foot.

In the car, though, I crossed my fingers. I mixed them up as much as I could, and waited behind my father's back, and beside my brother reading the face of his watch. Outside the window, the sky widened and lowered. The lid of one eye. One more. This was not new, this closing; this was the same stepping off any child knows, the same pushing and pushing of both feet into the floor of the car when the door shuts; and it is impossible to count how many children there have been, elsewhere, always, under such skies, or any others—buoyant expansive skies, striated no-telling skies, any purple or green-gray skies—who said nothing, not one word, but shut their eyes when cars they would not have entered for the world drew up to the curb and took them off, never home.

3

You can see her, my father said.

Where is she now?

In the hospital. She's in the hospital. Your Aunt Sarah's there, she'll take Jonas home. You can see your mother.

All right, I said. And I said to myself, I can see my mother. It was a simple chant, and I did see her, as I had seen her, in the morning at her desk. I see her from the kitchen door, from the back. She wears a blue bathrobe and reads her papers, sitting cross-legged, awkwardly, on a dining room chair, leaning over the desk, with her elbows pointing out. Her hair is uncombed and it hangs, swoops over the sides of her face. I can't see her face.

It may be a stroke, my father said.

Stroke, Jonas said.

It may be, my father said.

A word my mother could take to. Or not. She could say, Stroke, do you hear the finality, very simple. Slash. A paint stroke, the stroke of a pen. There. Effective as lightning, that is the simplest of all. Lightning strikes. Lucky strikes. Lightning never strikes twice. Stroke must never suggest caress, unless it's the sweeping, distracted stroke on the back of somebody's cat. There, kitty. Keep at a distance from such words, they're not ours. Stroke is the word of God's creation, not

ours. A stroke, it's done. Nothing's the same as before. Try
it. Put a stroke on a page, and there it is. Two strokes, it's
something else. Nothing's the same as before.

4   On the sidewalk outside the hospital, my father
takes my brother's hand, but he doesn't take mine. I am as
tall as he is.

Jonas, he says, Aunt Sarah will drive you home and stay
with you until we come along, do you understand?

Then my father sees us, his children in costume, his son a
mockery of a man, in a little gray suit, a vest, a watch stuck
in his fist; his daughter grown old, outlandish, with red bandanna, pasty red lips, earrings.

Can I wait here? My brother hangs back.

No, my father says. Inside, wait in the lobby. He opens
the glass door for us. I'll bring Aunt Sarah down. Andrea
Doria, fix your hair. Hurry up. Hurry, in there.

In the lavatory, I look in the mirror first, bringing my head
around, slowly, to see myself. If my mother turned in her
chair and looked over her shoulder, over the nap of the blue
robe, she would see this, too. Her voice would say, Dovie,
but gypsies are dark. This morning, in fact, my mother said
that.

The piece of cloth tied on my head, I take it off. A bit of
color, the scarf works like magic; it disappears, like the gauze
of a prayer cap, a white one, in daylight, mild as a halo. I
fold the bandanna and leave it on the washbowl. I take off the

earrings next. Wetting a brown paper towel, I wash at my lips. I wipe the lipstick with a dry towel and then wash again with the wet towel, soaped. I throw my hair over my head and comb it out, then throw it back. Looking in the mirror, head-on, I watch my eyes while I braid, by feel, one loose, quick braid. I roll it up like a rug at the base of my neck and pin it down. Even so, the face I see in the mirror, which my mother will see, looks like a cousin's face, somebody surely related to me, but larger, the forehead, the jaw more taut, and the eyes—oh, the eyes looking out never blink; they are drawn eyes, with indistinct shadows of purple, not makeup, beneath them. I look away from myself, as my mother would look away, her shoulder steering, her eyes headed towards a window, or the frosted pane on the lavatory door, this door metal and painted yellow, with a chrome handle that presses down.

Wait now, my father says. He waves to Jonas, in a plastic-covered chair in the lobby. Jonas sits with his legs straight out, the soles of his leather shoes showing.

On the elevator my father tells me, She just collapsed. She was ahead of me, we were walking out the walk, and she just fell. I thought she twisted her ankle, the way she buckled, but it's worse than that, Andrea Doria. The doctors say it is luck she's alive. They can't explain it. These things burst and you just have to start where you are. There's some paralysis, that's what comes with these things. They're used to this, they'll tell us more after the tests. She's not herself yet, but she's out of danger.

I want to tell my father, what are you talking about, she's never been out of danger. In the part of her brain, rushed with blood, her mind would have buoyed itself, and ridden through. If she's lost from sight for a moment, she'll surface; she'll hold her breath and dive and just when we start to worry, she'll show up, off to the side. She'll let an arm or a leg go limp; she'll give herself up to a float; she knows how to float.

It's Room 102, my father says. She might not know you.

Aunt Sarah knows me. Andrea, she says, your poor mother. She stands beside the bed, a pillar, my mother's attendant. She walks towards me, rustling in the Mennonite dress with the orthodox bibbed front and long skirt, to the ankles. The closer she gets, the more blurred she is—blond eyebrows, light brown hair snagged at the ears, uncolored lips; there are no lines between one part of her face and another. Your poor mother, she'd want to see you.

I see her, I say.

My mother is asleep, a sheet tucked nearly up to her neck, and one arm, with a clear tube attached, rests on the sheet. Her head is turned severely to one side on the pillow, I should straighten it out. But I sit on a chair beside the bed and I take her hand, what else can I do? In the hallway, I hear my father and Aunt Sarah talk about supper, five thirty, six o'clock, and talk of suitcases and what can be found in which closets. I hear their words. And I also hear, out of my mother's mouth, her vocal and involuntary breath: *Uh*, she says, a quick gasp in her throat; then *Shhhh*, a long hushing out through the teeth. *Shhh*. She is my mother; she'll keep me quiet.

I listen to her. *Uh*. I gasp with her. Waiting. *Sh. Shhh*.

I touch each of her fingers. I count them. And then, because she would want it, I look at her face, although it is turned so far into the pillow I know I will see only one eye, one ear.

It's Dovie, I'm right here. It's me.

Her eyelid is not completely closed, and the eye shows a half moon of white. You sleep, I tell her. I put two fingers on her eyelid and press it shut. My mother turns her head towards me, a fitful roll of her head that settles her hair deeper into the pillow. Both eyes are closed now, but her mouth, with the lips slightly apart, begins new sound with every breath. At one corner of her lips, a drop of saliva collects, wells there, and finally rolls down the side of her face. I am right here, I say.

But it's clear from the disappearance of color from her face, the discrepancies in the sounds of her voice, that she is away, she is somewhere else, gone into whatever hiding there is when the world flies apart and scatters itself out of reach. She's on her own, and she can't take me.

I'm right here, I say. You go ahead and sleep.

I know that crying is no help to her, so I don't even mention it. I hold her fingers and keep talking. I know she likes to listen to talk, so I keep talking. I'm right here.

What do you want to know? I ask her. I'll tell you everything.

Three

1 The message on Jonas's cake was Happy Birthday, with a red icing 10 underneath. My father carried the cake into the room, with the candles lighted, and we sang, and my mother, in her wheelchair at the end of the table, lifted her left arm, almost conducting. Her lips moved apart and together, not just in the measured movement of exercises, but randomly, lopsidedly, in an effort to shape the words she must have known we were singing. When we were finished, she nodded her head, so heartily I heard vertebrae in her neck crack.

Ssss, she said, her sound to bring someone close. Jonas went to her chair, and she used her good arm to pull his head down. Ssss, ssss, she said to the rest of us. And then with a deep breath, extending her lips, she said, Sho, sho. And more slowly, Sho, cho, cho. She pushed her index finger against Jonas's nose. Cho, she said. Jo.

Yes, Jonas! he said to her. I'm *Jonas*.

She opened her mouth and squinted her left eye, laughing. Jo. Ssss. Jo. Jo. Ssss. She held his arm and kept his ear close, practicing over and over. My father sat at the end of the table and ate his cake. I tried to eat, but the cake turned to crumb in my mouth, my jaw worked so hard with hers, and chocolate was not the taste I knew she was tasting. Jonas stayed with her, saying each time she made a sound, Yes, yes, Jonas, Jonas.

After a while, she let go his arm, and repeated, almost in a whisper, the two syllables, drawn together, Jone—Ssss. Jone—Iss.

Andrea Doria, come here, Jonas said. Did you hear that?

Yes, I heard. It was very clear.

Who's this? Jonas said to my mother, pointing to me. Who's that?

My mother said, Ssss. She looked at me, with her new face—askew, slung to the side; with her new gaze—one eye clear and piercing, the other wandering, drifting, and never settling where it aimed. I stared back and said, as I'd said hundreds of times for a month, It's me, Dovie. Dovie.

Mommy, try it, Jonas said. You're doing great. That's Andrea Doria. See her?

Don't tire your mother out, my father said. You can't hurry these things.

My mother slipped a little in her chair. I helped her upright and wiped her mouth.

It's Andrea Doria, Jonas said to my mother. See. Andrea Doria. Andrea, he said. Andrea.

My mother opened her mouth. Eh, she said. Eh. Eh.

Yes! Jonas said. That's it. *Andrea.*

End, my mother said. End. She coughed the sounds out. End—y.

Andrea! Yes! my brother said. That's Andrea Doria.

And—y, my mother said. And—y.

She knows you, my brother said. She's saying your name, too.

I said, Jonas, I'll put her to bed now. She's worn out. Eat your cake, too. You haven't had your cake.

Do you think she'll be talking soon? my brother asked my father.

You can hear that she will. Certainly she will.

I wheeled my mother to the bathroom, undressed her, and washed her arms, her feet. I exercised her legs for her, and her arms. You are doing wonderful, I told her. Keep working, you're doing better every day.

Andy, she said.

I'm Dovie, I told her. But her eyes were closing.

I put her nightgown on her and wheeled her to the bed and lifted her in. Ssss, she said. The next moment, she was asleep.

I can do that, my father said from the doorway.

She's very light. I'm taller than she is now. It's all right.

You and Jonas hoe the west field tomorrow, will you? Aunt Sarah takes your mother in for the therapy, she won't need you here.

I'll ask Marlene, too, I said.

I kissed my mother on the forehead, and my father kissed her, too. It's been the worst month there is, he said. I don't know where we're headed. But you've been a help. Your mother would be proud.

I miss her, I told him.

Not here. Not in here, he said.

We walked into the hallway and shut the door, and I leaned my head against the plaster of the wall, cool and more fragrant than anything in the open air. The wall smelled of rock and roots, the ones uncovered in the dark. I pressed my forehead against the wall; I tried to breathe without making a sound.

Across the hallway, my father leaned his back against the

wall and let himself slip down until he was sitting on the floor.

She doesn't remember anything. I'd know it, I said.

She'll come around, my father said. You can see. It's slow, but she's getting better. This is the way it goes, that's what the doctors say. It's harder on us, they say that. You've talked to them. You know as much as I do here. Just look ahead. We're getting there.

Jonas turned on the hall light, but as soon as he saw us, he turned it off. He smelled like chocolate cake; when he came close to me, his hair smelled like cake.

She said some words, I can't believe it, he said. I'll teach her more in the morning.

You do that, I said. I put my arms around him; it had to be done, although it was not solace, but an act of solace, an act. Each muscle worked and moved as it should, while an equal lassitude worked against it, and strength was a doubled-back effort, annihilating.

Here was a strength my mother had never applauded. She'd left it out of all her accounts, never gave it a nod. It was something she would have thrown back at God, and said, This is for *you*, this is *your* sort of muscle.

2   Marlene Beecher brought gifts for my mother. Whenever she came into the living room and walked towards my mother's chair to say hello, my mother automatically reached

out and pulled at Marlene's hands, hidden behind her back. Marlene would pretend to struggle a moment, and then she'd give up some small ribboned box which my mother would tear open with her fingernails. It was usually a windup toy of some kind, a jumping gorilla, a kangaroo that flipped itself over, or a magnet to put on the refrigerator—a strawberry magnet, or an Amish girl magnet.

I told Marlene one afternoon, You're giving my mother baby presents. She's not a baby.

Honey, she's had a bad time. Those things perk her up, you can see that. If she doesn't like them, she can throw them away.

We were working together on the two-seated tobacco cultivator, pulled by the tractor, with Jonas driving. The work took both hands, moving the cultivator tines in and out, between the tobacco plants. The exhaust from the tractor blew over us, and my back ached, my head ached. The plants drifted by, between our legs, and I counted them, into the hundreds, hypnotically.

I face facts, Marlene said. You should face facts, too, honey. After what your mother's been through, if she's not the same, you have to accept who she is. She's your mother. She might not be the same as before, but she's here and her mind works, and she sees what's going on. You can't snap her back to exactly what she was. Anyway, look how *you've* changed. She probably doesn't remember you as a little girl. You two can start a new life. Anyway, every mother and daughter break off at your age, stroke or no stroke. My mother nearly threw me out of the house when I was fourteen, and this was the same woman who saved me from drowning in Coatesville.

She saved you from drowning?

I was a dumb kid, Marlene said. Every kid is a dumb kid. In back of our apartment building was a city pool, and neglect is neglect, you know that. In the fall when it rained they didn't drain it, somebody didn't drain it, and then it froze one night and in the morning I decided to go skating, in my sneakers, of course. There wasn't much water, a few feet. But the ice gave, and I went under. My mother said she heard a splash and thought, there, some dumb kid has fallen into that water. She looked out and recognized my red cap and she ran down seven flights of stairs just spinning around the turns, with her hand on the ball of the wooden railing. She said she beat the elevator, easy. And then she strode into the water and pulled me out, and blew air into my mouth. And I came to. The mayor gave her a medal, which, by the way, she threw in my face when I was fourteen. How old are you?

Twelve.

You look fourteen.

I'm twelve.

Well, don't worry about your mother. She got through the worst part, and now we just have to help her live her life the best way she can. It's her life, you know. Take her out to the prison. Johnny Smoke can show her the new lake.

When she can walk, I will, I said.

That's when I knew she would walk. You hear yourself saying a thing, and you hear what you know.

It didn't take long. The next week, my mother could stand. Several times a day, she'd call me over with a sudden gesture, her left hand in a fist, circling, and I'd help her stand up. She didn't attempt to go anywhere; we just stood together in front of her chair until her knees gave and she sank back, and breathed hard with her lips together, a sound like *humpf*.

In the kitchen one morning, she made a fist and said the word *garden*.

Garden? You want to see the garden?

She leaned back her head and pulled in a mouthful of air, then parted her lips on the left side of her face and, with great force, hissed, *Yes!*

I wheeled her outside and down the hill to the edge of the garden. She wanted to stand, and with much less trouble than usual, she pulled herself upright, using my arm for a light support. She stood a long time, pointing her arm towards each row of plants, sometimes nodding her head and other times shaking it. Pulling at my arm, she took a few steps towards the tobacco field, off to the side of the garden, but she wasn't paying attention to the tobacco plants, which were fully grown, their tops reaching over her head.

She pointed instead at the ground, saying, Dare, dare, or There, there.

What is it?

There! she said.

In the ditch at the edge of the field was a groundhog hole. That's all I could see.

That? You mean that groundhog hole?

Yes! Her face was red with the explosive sounds of the word.

They're everywhere, I said. I found a hole at the top of the hill between here and the prison. Maybe a lookout.

Yes! she said. Yes!

But she sounded angry, as if she were really saying no! and I looked at her face, and that's what it was.

It's all right. They haven't bothered the garden.

Yes! she shouted. She jabbed towards the hole with her arm, punching with her fist.

I'll fill it in. It'll be dug out in the morning, but I'll fill it in. All right?

Yes!

I felt her weight on my arm ease, and I helped her back to the chair.

With an interest she hadn't shown in months, she watched while I filled in the hole, first with rocks, and then with shovelfuls of dirt. I set a big rock on top.

On the way back to the house, my mother dropped her head to one side, shut her eyelids, and seemed to doze. When we reached the porch, I lifted her into her lounge chair, and she opened her eyes and shook her head, Andy, yes, she said. Yes.

It was hard for me to look at her, but I did. I tried to imagine, in the rooms behind her eyes, the sound of a long speech unfolding, echoing there, any number of words. There should have been rooms full of crumpled paper. But her eyes closed and she rocked her head, closing up in sleep. She'd managed to fool herself, not just me. Somewhere, out of sight, she'd hoarded everything. She'd stowed away and shipped out. Like God holed up with himself, about all she could prove for now was, everything's in the dark.

3

Out of the blurred wash of October, the morning fogs that sieved themselves through the screen of the back porch and fell apart there in rows of droplets, out of that kind of early diffuseness, appeared the charcoal shape, first the arms, both arms, then the rest of the body of my father.

His arms reached out, and he opened the door to the porch.

I couldn't have said with any surety where he had been, but he hadn't walked far, not with his shoes flecked with moisture, one or two sprays kicked up, not with his face clean as fine cloth, unlabored.

He stepped into the kitchen and wiped his shoes. His brown hair lay at his neck, the color of leaves.

What day was that?

He was shaped like a man. He was dressed like a man.

4 Marlene Beecher and Johnny Smoke brought my mother a TV, and my father said, All right, she will enjoy it. Is that all right with you kids?

We put it on the coffee table, a big box, in front of my mother's chair. Like any outsider, my mother was exempt from all our rules: she owned a TV, she drank a juice glass of brandy at night, she wore a zippered robe. She sat in a special chair that adjusted to several settings with a left-hand control.

During a commercial on TV one evening, my mother turned herself in the chair and said to me, Andy, write a note. I'm writing to Ruth.

Ruth had sent postcards once a week since my mother's stroke, and I had sent postcards back, a few sentences on her condition, her progress. But this was the first time my mother wanted to write.

She said, Andy, get some nice paper.

I'm set, I said. I put a sheet of typing paper in the typewriter.

Not that. Get notepaper. This is a real letter.

I found a small sheet of yellow paper edged with twists of red, and I rolled it into the typewriter. I sat at the dining room table, and my mother dictated the letter from her reclining chair, which propped up her legs and leaned her backwards.

Dear Ruth, she said, and I typed Dear Ruth on the notepaper.

December 20, 1968. Put the date next, Andy. Now go on. Say, Andy is typing this letter for me. I do not use a pen well.

Dear Ruth,

December 20, 1968. Andy is typing this letter for me. I do not use a pen well. The worst trouble is my right leg. Yes. The doctor is pleased.

We have prepared Christmas. Andy the cookies, Jonas a cake in the freezer. The tree is up. It is busy. I am tired of it, but Sarah does my work, too. I want to hear about Christmas in France. You write and Andy reads your letters, that will be fine. I cannot see words yet. I see writing but not the words. That will come it is said. You are my dearest friend. I would rather see your face. Ruth, Ruth. Yours truly.

That's it, my mother said.

Do you want me to write that's it?

Yes. That's the end. Write it last.

Shall I put your name?

Put X.

You want to put an X? You could do that.

No, *you* put X. She'll know it's me.

And so I typed the ending the way she wanted.

> Yours truly. That's it.
>
> X

5 Aunt Sarah slept on the daybed. I tried to wake before she did, but I couldn't do it. My father's older sister, she rose first, always, before light, got herself dressed and brushed and sweetened with soap. She used a special amber bar of soap that she kept on a saucer in the bathroom, separate from our soap dish. She wanted us to think of her stay as temporary. With my mother, Aunt Sarah pretended that she'd always lived in the house, helping us out; that nothing was different, that she was at home. But with Jonas and me, she pretended her visit was short-term, a vacation, just about up. If she needed to find a pitcher for milk, she took Jonas and me into a separate room and asked quietly, Can either of you help me out here? She made a point of letting us know she was new, unfamiliar with our household. She kept a suitcase packed by the daybed. As soon as your mother's able to cope, she said, you won't have to put up with me.

After breakfast, while Jonas and I collected our books for school, my mother and Aunt Sarah sat at the kitchen table and finished their cinnamon tea.

You should be exercising more, Aunt Sarah said. The Lord needs you whole.

I'm whole enough, my mother said. I'm whole.

Well, I worry, Aunt Sarah said. We want you strong.

If we're going to worry, my mother said, let's worry about Jonas and Andy.

Nobody needs to worry about us, I said. I stuffed some sandwiches in brown paper bags. Jonas wrapped carrot sticks in waxed paper, and I packed those, too.

We're in good shape, Jonas said.

Children always need worrying over, Aunt Sarah said. No child grows up without giving the gift of gray hair to parents.

They seem so shy, my mother said. She talked as if we weren't there to hear.

Of course they're shy, that's fine. Rather have them shy and a little inward than out there stirring up trouble. Be thankful they're shy.

They need other children to play with, my mother said. Maybe they're working too much, we should think about that. We could make some plans for a party with children or something.

Work never hurt children, Aunt Sarah said.

We're doing fine, I said. Forget the party.

We don't need a party, Jonas said.

Do you hear that? Forget the party, my mother said. All right. No more about it, if that's how it is.

Children who don't want parties! Aunt Sarah laughed.

You see what I mean? my mother said. Then she laughed, too, a light-headed, dizzying laugh, a brand-new one, that took her and held her, like a siege of hiccups, until her face flushed and her lips clamped shut, muffling the sound and quieting it.

Who's upsetting who? my father asked, coming into the kitchen in his white shirt and overalls.

Nobody's upset, Aunt Sarah said. Laughter's the best medicine.

We're just laughing, my mother said.

At the counter, my father poured a cup of coffee and handed Jonas and me money for milk at school.

We're steaming the seedbeds today, he told us. By the time you get home, there won't be much to see but the muslin.

We'll miss it? Jonas cried.

You'll miss the bus, Aunt Sarah said. Get along.

Bye, bye, said my mother. She was still laughing, her eyes squinting up and watering.

Outside, I shifted my books and bent my head down and smelled my forearm. I told Jonas, If you breathe in, your arm smells like the steamer. Try it.

In April, for the tobacco seedbeds, they brought in a steam engine to sterilize the ground. They laid out large metal plates on the soil and pumped the steam under them, into the ground. Tobacco seed, fine as pepper, practically a dust itself, couldn't compete with weed seeds, or anything, and the steamer guaranteed ideal conditions, nothing else there.

Jonas sniffed his forearm. What sort of party were they talking about?

There's no party. That was just talk.

We're going to miss the steamer, Jonas said.

That would be a party, I said, and Jonas nodded.

I pushed my arm, back and forth, under my nose, and smelled the singed air and soil, a stretch of ground so pure that when the sun hit it, only one thing would grow.

Anybody could point to the first leaves under the muslin and say, There, that's tobacco, it's nothing else. And we grow it for no good reason, the same as we grow this girl.

6 My father's arms changed visibly.

In public, he assumed the cross-armed posture of anyone else's father. His forearms covered his breasts and flattened the pockets of his shirts, in momentary pause. But he couldn't hold his arms still. He couldn't lean back for long against a wall to talk.

When he picked Jonas and me up at school, the weeks of the first tobacco planting without my mother's help, he waited at the door of the car, lounging with the other fathers and grandfathers, but his shoulders worked all the while at arranging his arms. He maneuvered and placed his legs, too. He rolled up his sleeves as if his forearms were even now in the afternoon light expanding, thickening, and when he moved his arms in hello, his forearms did seem to grow, wondrous—limbless bodies of themselves, the fingers slight as feathers. Those arms, those two distinct bodies he'd loosened, like his own children, gave him whatever they could of a leaping and diving through the air, and he let them fly.

Other men, at rest in their stillness, talked loudly. But my father, whose words seemed to stall and hush in his chest, released his arms, and they soared and pointed through space, where the muscle and skin and hair, where the heat of the whole body, traveled.

7 My mother said she was determined to shoot something. She'd had enough.

Aunt Sarah had explained to her how dried blood, or wet blood, too, she supposed, was known to deter animals. Aunt Sarah knows so much, my mother said, I'm only taking her advice. Stay in the house if it scares you, Andy.

I turned my back and walked out to the barn.

My mother did her own shopping now, and her first trip out, she came home with a rifle. Wrapped in brown paper, it looked like a single oar from a rowboat, and she carried it awkwardly, dipping the thing like an oar. It makes me sick, she said, these groundhogs, I don't think we have a choice. The question is, whose garden is it?

She lay the package down on the kitchen table and unwrapped it. I saw the sheen of the barrel first and then the waxed wood, very dark, of the stock. The plan isn't to kill, of course, she said, but to strike fear. She giggled. This is a noisemaker. I am sick of being *their* gardener. There's nothing wrong with that. There are times when action makes more sense than no action, you can see that.

She rolled the rifle back into the paper and said, Andy, don't tell your father. This goes in the closet.

Although my father was miles away at the other farm, my mother tiptoed into the kitchen closet and hid the rifle under the winter coats. You swear not to tell? she said, and I nodded. Good! This is my job, don't you think? She smiled, then laughed again. A drop of saliva began to slip from the side of her mouth, and she frowned and reached across the table to me. Hand me a hanky, Andy.

She wiped her lips and blotted them. How is that now, Andy? How do I look?

8

Whenever my mother talked, the places around her, inside, out of doors, each person, the simplest objects—cup, cloth, lips, cloud—stabilized, solidified. Nothing was called into doubt. Nothing escaped. There was much laughter, and sometimes a casual walking from set to set, the rooms of the house lit up first here, then there, as a stage lights up, left or right, one cubicle after the other, then the middle, an inset room, then the background, a slope to the new lake.

When we visited the prison, my mother and I walked from the house, between the fields, on a direct line into the woods to the edge of our property, where the prison wall adjoined our land. In the locust woods, we followed the wall the long way, around to the main gate. With one hand, I held my mother's elbow, guiding her; but I let my other hand hang back and scrape along the rocks, in and out, rock to mortar, mortar to rock. I'd often wondered if the warden had been one of my mother's three men—the father, or possibly the son; but my mother had never named names. I'd never known how to ask. I'd decided on my own, out of a child's grim definitive ordering, that one was the farmer, one the warden, and one—who knows?—a con man or ex-con. My mother had

had overlapping loyalties. She'd had ideas that cut both ways, like illegal knives. She might have managed to love a warden as well as a felon. But I couldn't be certain.

That's right, my mother used to say, about ordinary confusions. You *can't* be certain.

I reminded my mother we used to walk this way often. When I was little, I said. Do you remember?

I remember all that I have to, my mother said. And so should you. You don't think we've come through all this for nothing! You've got a fine future, remember that. I want to be proud of you, and I will be. You won't disappoint me.

She looked ahead on the path and tossed her head, so that her hair flicked around—a shaking off of peripheral matters.

I know my Andy, she said. And my eye is on her future.

She touched her left eye and pointed forward. She laughed her new laugh, high-pitched. It rippled and stopped; it stuck like a flag at the end of her talk, and it said, *nonsense.* Against her will, because she always frowned, it said, now, I have finished with *that.*

Johnny Smoke met us at the gate and led us past the blockhouses, across a green courtyard, and into the grounds near the far wall, where a new path cut through the scrubland, a path marked clearly with a diver's form burned into posts.

My mother walked steadily. Johnny Smoke pointed ahead and promised my mother, You'll see, they hauled some white sand up from Tampa!

And then we were there, at a wide, lapping lake, a blue bowl of water, with a white beach, a dock.

I see it, my mother said.

On the beach, my mother bent her knees and sat down. She waved to a couple of swimmers, staff or prisoners, it was hard to tell, far off on a raft, anchored where the lake had been dredged deep, Johnny Smoke explained, guaranteeing cool water through August.

Make yourself at home, Johnny said. I'll check the dock.

My mother sat with her back straight and watched the swimmers. Tell me, she said, not looking at me, what you are doing at school.

My mother knew what was fitting and legitimate to ask. She'd mastered a protocol, and she knew which surroundings, which events, to ignore. Let a lake appear. No matter.

While I told her about school, she pushed her left hand, which was still her best hand, through the white sand; she sifted handfuls. Where the sand had been kicked up, heaped with sticks and leaves, she dug in, and out of one clump she yanked a dollar bill, folded in half.

Andy! she said.

She unfolded the bill and ironed it out on her thigh.

Here, she said. You put that in the bank! She laughed her rapid-fire laugh, then frowned.

Without help from me, she pulled her body forward in the sand, closer to the water, and kept digging where the lake, no doubt days ago, had sprawled in wind and pushed ashore heaps of debris.

That's one! she said. I bet there's another.

9   I thought I could understand why my mother, having pulled herself back, would fold and label and rearrange

all that she could. But she said, with a switch of complaint in her voice, that she wanted an orderly house, as if she could guess we had lived for years in disarray. When she and Aunt Sarah opened a closet door to go at it, they spoke with surprise and with an uncomprehending pity in their tones about the mix-up in winter and summer clothes, about the hangers that lay on the floor with the shoes, in dust.

One rainy week, we spent several days cleaning the stripping room and firing up the stove with my mother's old papers. She pulled out the boxes from under the sizing table, and she read through several of Ruth's letters. My mother remarked how silly we sound in letters, so wrapped up in the moment. What we have here, she said, is melodrama. You can't trust words on a page, can you? Ruth could say anything she wanted, my mother said. It's nice to keep in touch, she said, but the minute you start believing what somebody writes, long distance, you might as well point to your head and say to the world, look at a fool, look right here.

Sorting through the boxes, I kept an eye out for my mother's blue marble, the swirled one, but I didn't see it. When I thought about asking, where's the good-luck marble you used to carry, where's the Beauty, I couldn't say a word. I looked at the room, at the boxes we'd already emptied, and I must have slumped, heavily, against the table.

My mother heard me and shook her head, laughing her own laugh. Unbelievable, she said. This is unbelievable. What a mess.

She made it her habit to throw out letters as they arrived, but nevertheless, she continued to have me type her responses to Ruth. She dictated humdrum accounts of the weather, all the details about the lake, the new landscaping. And Ruth's letters came back, mirror letters—matter-of-fact, with parallel descriptions of France's weather, of Dol and its ramparts, which reminded her, she said, of the walls of the penitentiary.

After I read these letters to my mother, no matter what Ruth had written, my mother would say, Yes, that sounds very nice. Pitch that out now, and get the notepaper, Andy. We'll write back.

Soon Ruth began adding a P.S.—A.D., and I responded with my own, P.S.—Dear Ruth. In her postscripts, Ruth wrote about her researches into the *lais* of Marie de France; and she wrote about her dreams, if they included me or my mother—her clear dreams, she called them. She said that the farther away she traveled, the clearer her dreams became. She said since she'd been in France, her dreams were astonishingly sharp, all the objects and details within them precisely focused. In these dreams, Ruth said she could pick up an object and look it over, forwards and backwards, up and down, into every hollow or facet, knowing she'd never again see so well. In one dream, she said my mother handed her a cut-glass vase and an apple, and she saw them completely, particularly, *wholly*, in all of their colors and shadows. It took many minutes to see what was there, there was so much. In another one of her clear dreams, Ruth said she was listening to my mother, and my mother's voice, her early voice, turned to undifferentiated sound and then to streams of color, flowing from between her lips. The words were no longer words, but light and sound, cascading.

I wrote to Ruth about my dreams, too, even the ordinary ones. Once, soon after I'd been through it, I mentioned the nightmare I'd often had—a long, lengthening dream of my mother drowning. I thought she'd be interested. I told Ruth

how my own eyes went under with my mother, and how I
saw what my mother saw until she closed her eyes.

10

It's no good, my mother said.

She was peeling potatoes for supper, and I was setting the
table.

I can see it already, she said, they won't scare. You would
think, wouldn't you, that gunfire would reach a high pitch in
their ears and give a shock. It's supposed to be a terrible sound,
isn't it? But no. Not at all.

She set a peeled potato on the cutting board and sliced once,
right through.

I have no intention, she said, of feeding the whole animal
kingdom. Traps don't work, scarecrows don't work, gunfire
doesn't. You saw it, they just turn around and come back.
Gunfire doesn't scare.

It scares me, I said.

My mother looked at me. Andy, she said, try to stand a
little straighter. You slump. That's it. You're pretty enough
for anybody to see, don't fold yourself up. A straight back
is an important thing in this world, you should be able to
see that. People who look at their toes might as well fold
up and die. But Marlene, there, now think of her, how she
stretches her neck when she talks, that's a good sign, she can
meet people head-on and talk to them. Watch how she nods,
straight up and down, people like to have her around. Try

to look like you're put together right, that's the key. Tuck your shirt in.

What will you do with the gun? I asked her.

Nothing. What *should* I do? It's put away. Anyway, Andy, the purpose of a gun is to shoot, right? If I get it out, I might as well try it.

For me, then, it wasn't a surprise when I came in from the field the next day, ahead of my father, to see that my mother had set up two straw bales as her target, drawn a bull's-eye on a sheet of paper, and arranged two chairs some distance away, one chair to sit on, one as a prop for the gun. On the ground at her side lay a pamphlet on target practice, open to a chart of instructions.

She fired, and straw flew from the bale.

She adjusted the chairs, took aim, and fired again.

At the second shot, my father ran around the side of the barn. My mother stood up, the rifle rising.

My father's arms, both of them, flew upward. He stopped where he was, but his arms kept going, circling, the arms of a man tricked and deserted, who reaches up, grapples empty air, and lets it take him.

11

P.S.—A.D., You must tell me, what does your mother see, going under?

12 The word was, she is recovered.

Everyone said so. And knowing the silence she'd stumbled into, having lifted often enough the shapeless, sinking air that had fallen across her shoulders, I said, too, to anyone asking the question, Yes, she's recovered. It's been a comeback.

Because there she was, choosing her clothes out of the closet and putting them on, walking in and out of the house, driving the car, talking freely: I'm wearing this green dress today, I haven't worn this one for a while. Andy, what do you think?

She turned around and around, a little spin that looked mechanical.

There was a quickness and sharpness in my mother's motions that diminished her actions and clipped her words. She was skittery. Having lost some time, she speeded up. And moving fast, she seemed random; often she opened doors one after the other with the impatience of someone convinced she'd arrived at the wrong place at the right time.

Usually I managed to think the one simple thought: my mother has lost weight. She dissolved herself, bodily, which allowed her the amazing social trick of appearing or disappearing in a room, effortlessly. But her mind darted, too. She lit on one topic, spun there, and then through a process that seemed like buffeting, she skewed off somewhere else.

I was the large one in the house, the new giant. And like a creature overgrown, I was afraid even a slight gesture—the swing out of my arms when I yawned, a clap of hands with surprised laughter—might damage something inside her, where I couldn't see. Or break the series of dams she'd constructed, and my mother would be swept away in that flood.

13 During the summer, my brother grew past me, each month setting the bones of his face at more of an angle and opening the bowls of his ears into wider, more cavernous amphitheaters. His ears decorated his head, artfully engineered lobes, sculpted, the principal sights to be seen, not ruins or curiosities out of the way. My brother registered sounds, the wholeness of words. He didn't have to turn his head. And his own voice picked up a range of reverberations; it rolled out from the hollows of his chest. It rang with authority, propelled as it was from the center of the brain, between the two ears. When he left for summer camp, my mother kissed him good-bye, and she held not his shoulders but his ears in her hands, and she drew his head downward.

Jonas's girl friends at camp, if there were girl friends, would have touched his ears first, then touched his hands, I knew that. And when he came back from camp, although his hair had grown longer, it separated front and back, around the ears, and my mother, of course, kissed the right ear and then the left ear before her usual kiss hello, hard on the forehead.

We have a project, she told him on the way to the house. The campaign starts tomorrow.

My mother explained to Jonas and me that it was out of hand, completely, and now was the time to do something.

Her project concerned the groundhogs, the babies that had grown up.

In the morning, at the edge of the garden, she said, There are half a dozen babies and now they are out *here*. I want you two to sit here on either side of the garden, you're my lookouts, she said, you're my sentinels. Sentinels.

The word, and her ease with saying it, made her laugh. She stopped walking and bent over at the waist to laugh. When she stood straight, the laugh came up with her, and she threw her head back, cutting the sound loose.

I looked at Jonas, and yes, he was listening. Catching everything. He was not saying anything. Not laughing. Nobody could join in my mother's laughter.

Don't look so sour, Andy, my mother said. What if your face froze that way? Stand up straight now, and let's get *to* this.

What do we do? Jonas asked.

Nothing, my mother said. You just stand at the edge of the garden and wait. You stand there, you freeze, and wait there, and wait there, until they come out, and they will in this sun, and then you slip to the side, to cut off their run back to that hole, or that one. She pointed to one side and then to the other, where the groundhogs had heaped up dirt outside two tunnel entrances. *You* cut them off, confuse them a moment, and *I* take advantage and . . . *dispatch* them! Andy, over there. Jonas, this side. While they get used to *you*, she said, and she spun around, her usual twirl, *I'll* get the gun.

Jonas squatted at his edge of the garden and fiddled with some leaf scraps in the soil. I squatted down, too, back in the weeds. The air shimmered between us. The garden's heat swelled there and lifted and shoved its weight onto my shoulders; there was so much heat, wave after wave, that the air collapsed, burdensome, hot on the slopes of the cheek, hot in the throat. Jonas's ears went red, and he wiped at the moisture above his lip; he wiped his chin. His hands were dirty and his face smudged. I watched his breathing, steady, in pace with my breathing at first, but then it picked up and went shallow. By slight bodily shifts, adjustments of thought, we were both working a camouflage, complicated as the heat closing around. Our job was, blend in. Disappear.

From where I was, close to the ground, within the rim of pigweed, I thought, when my mother comes back and braces the gun against her shoulder, I'll be able to see her lips above the barrel. That may be all I'll see. She'll look around and her lips will say the words, All right, all right, where *are* you two?

14 My mother's face softened, and rounded at the edges. First the right side, but after a while the whole of the left side, too, relaxed; and the lines under her eyes and at the corners of her mouth disappeared. She slept in the reclining chair in the early evenings, and when she woke, before she opened her eyes, she pressed the handle that straightened the chair, set her feet on the floor, and brought herself forward. When she opened her eyes, her face was serene, the face of a young woman, alert to the moment, and pleased with the ease of her coming back, out of nowhere into a lighted room.

Jonas, she said, read me the funnies.

My brother leafed through the newspaper.

Good, you are hard at work, she said to me, at the table with my geography. Andy, tell me, did we have dessert?

I tried to remember.

From his desk, where he kept the farm books, my father answered for me, We had ice cream, yes. Do you want some more?

That would be wonderful, my mother said. A small bowl, yes.

I learned to look at the maps in my book and play a trick with my eyes. Whatever was neat and clear on the page, I would smudge. If the map showed political boundaries in Central America, I'd fill in some jungles and mess the border lines with a smeared darkness of foliage. I could squint and let the Pacific Ocean roll itself into the coastal hills. If the map showed the Himalayas, I managed to shake my head, imperceptibly, and draw in my mind a cross-hatching of paths, migratory flyways, all kinds of windflow lines. I wanted to say out loud to my mother, you don't want to see too clearly. You don't want to see one thing at a time.

But I knew my mother's answer. Yes, you do.

My mother didn't want my advice. When she accepted an invitation to teach Bible school for two weeks, I said, Don't bother with me this year, I'm getting too old. But she signed me up, and said, Andy, you'll enjoy it. You'll have a good time.

On the way to church, my mother drove the car and I rode in the front seat. I heard her preparation. Jesus set himself goals, she said. One thing at a time. He got himself closer and closer to God, one step at a time. He brought people to him, little by little. Don't look back. God doesn't hide on the back roads. You go straight ahead, and the doors open, one after another. God opens doors. God paves the road.

We stepped out of the car in the parking lot, and it seemed a proof of her lesson. She smiled and slammed the door.

We assembled in the basement of the Mennonite church, around the rectangular tables, for Bible discussions, each table a different age group, with a different teacher. I liked this part, when the teachers reached up towards the ceiling and pulled at white curtains, like the curtains around a hospital bed, on curving rods, that surrounded each table. And we separated into white rooms, with soft blowy walls. I didn't mind any of it—the soap smell of my teacher, the sounds of her, crinkling her light summer dress, the scuff of her flat-heeled shoes on the concrete floor. My mother's group met at the very next table, behind the white curtain. And I sat on the side of our table nearest her, to listen. Through the curtain, I heard what she told her students. I paid close attention, while I kept my eyes on my own teacher, a quiet, dark-haired woman with thick eyebrows and a nose flattened out on the tip. With the curtains drawn around and the children hushed, there was little left but the sweetness of voices and the sounds of cloth, like wings, soft and muffled, always moving a little, as if someone, everyone, were attending to minor matters, simply attending.

I heard my mother pause to catch her breath. She inhaled. She said, Now, children, if you look at the picture in your books.

And without the book I saw the road, and Jesus and the little children—no houses in sight, no jungle, no men and women coming out of apartments.

But I filled those in, and I brought along bulldozers, too, and I sat Ruth on the sidelines, and filled in the shadows with every animal I could think of. And, for my mother's sake, I floated her naked up in the sky next to a male angel who carried his robes on his arm like a folded coat. I never covered them up with clouds.

My mother said, Look at the children on that path, they are following Jesus' footsteps. Where do you think they are going, boys and girls?

I shut my ears. And said to myself, Nobody knows, nobody knows, as many times as I had to until I could catch my mother saying, Absolutely, children. And then I would listen again.

It was easy, hearing her coaxing, high-pitched voice from the other side of the curtain, to disbelieve what she said and to picture my mother somewhere else, like God in his darknesses, wholly absent.

They were in their cave, those two, with its sweet fields and beaches, all the comforts of summer, talking all day and exclaiming sometimes to each other about Earth, still astonished: Who would have thought? Who would have ever dreamed?

15 I wrote to Ruth what she asked, no more. That was our rate of exchange, an equivalency, my mother the one in the balance. If my mother diminished in the house, in her new propriety, and let a hundred annoyances chisel away at her, Ruth and I, for our parts, kept her wholly to ourselves and let words refurbish her, as if an accounting could sustain her, and our muscles work for her, representative, and our minds. It was the painstaking, hoarding task of memory, filling the pages and tying up packing boxes, loading the attics, according to one credo, the sure geological one: lay things out where they lie, cover them there; give way when the rain arrives and let it sift its accumulations downward, because what we can finally know is no less than what was, which is: composition of rock.

And no composition is like another, Ruth wrote.

Tell me about Marie de France, I asked her. What have you found?

First, she wrote back, what does your mother see?

And so I told her.

My mother dives, not from shore, not from anywhere, straight through the surface of the ocean, into the watercolor blue, unstained, and she turns the waves under with her, a visible turmoil, but her dive proceeds, uninterrupted; she arrows down and scatters the air that clings to her, and it streams back, pearled along her arms and along the strands of her hair. Nobody sees her.

Except for me. And that is the dream of the dream: my seeing with my mother's eyes. As she dives deeper, the lighted world's efflorescence disperses behind her; and ahead, another brightness, more intense, more focused, rises out of the black below—a fireball, a fountain of light. My mother aims herself towards it and zeroes in. At the last moment, by inches, the paths stream apart, rush parallel, a pillar of fire on her left shooting upward with a force counter to the force of her descent. The pillar flames at the edges, and inside, it twirls and embroils itself with a central column of fire. Even with water falling upon it, the fire does not burn itself out, but rises and fuels and builds. The pillar of flames burns without oxygen, flaring, and by the same law, my mother, without air, breathes deeply and rockets downward.

She descends along the column of fire and she sees within it whatever is there. She does not shut her eyes, not from beginning to end.

By bending her hands at the wrists, braking her dive, my mother slows her descent, just enough to look at the shapes, portraits, in the fire. What else is there to see? All are pairs— mother and child, woman and man, two women, two men, a child and a child, another and another, this one and that one, sometimes two strangers scarcely aware of each other.

My mother rushes by and the column of fire surges with images until these begin to link and move by, a long strip of separate scenes, many frames of a film, but each one developed, and moving upward as if the roll were being wound through the fire and burning there, and not being burned and not extinguishing. My mother sees the exchanges of mind, the collaborations of innumerable souls; they are drenched with fire and they roll and roll, nothing stops them. The child stares through its father's fingers; mother and daughter sit at a table; on a narrow bed, a couple, lean as acrobats, collide; a crowned king is seated center, regal, while a young girl, all dressed up, draws a weapon and shoots.

They are brief scenes. And they wind away: two men with two glasses of wine; a father and his father, floating on their backs in a turquoise pool; two children crossing a desert, a gray desert; a couple posed at the door of a house. The details certifying time and place are not certain. Backgrounds shift. Objects appear clearly here, but there, veiled, obscured by shadow, they fail to define themselves.

One and one, says my mother, is one and one. She is talking to me.

We pass by a hundred faces. The darker the deeps of the

ocean become, the fuller the fire of the column, the more fluid and laden. The art of it complicates, as connections between the bodies become visible, a webbing; and something like spirits becomes apparent too, as fire within the fire, forming fabrics, pools of fabrics, immense magmas of fire within the fire.

My mother pulls in her arms, and propels them, sharp rotations, on each side. Here, her arms are both strong, equal in power, and her motions generate spirals, right and left, and out of the tips of these spirals, out of the tips of her fingers, shoot jets of blue flame. My mother watches the flames. Her body slows in the water. With slight kicks of her feet, she snaps out flames from her toes. At her knees, there are rings of fire; from her breasts, ribbons of flame. And out of her eyes, flame and flame.

We may be inside the column of fire, I don't know any more where we are. My mother's arms blur with the colors of fire. Her flesh stretches out, nubbed like canvas. And there I am, over there, a face like mine, painted with fire, flames on my lips. And then my mother closes her eyes.

16 She came down the hill towards us, her legs giving hardly at all. No one could say she limped. But she carried the gun badly, in both arms, cradling it like a board, a two-by-four, a stiffened acquaintance, wrapped up, the whole body varnished.

Behind two bales of straw, her blind, my mother positioned

herself, with the gun settled in a niche on top of the top bale, the gun's barrel obscured except for the black hollow of the bore, an open eye. There was another eye, one of my mother's, above the bale, too. She'd messed her hair, fluffed it around, so that the curls, about the color of straw, fell over her face. I knew she was back there. On the other hand, she seemed to withdraw, evaporate, into the heat of the air.

As usual, we weren't the culprits to abscond; she was.

Jonas and I, unarmed, were dug in, unsheltered, directly in her line of sight, doing her dirty work, luring her prey, waiting for some kind of sign from her telling us, *Now*, step out, *now*, cut them off, there, *now*, give me room for a clean shot.

And then she said, *Now*.

We jumped, flailed our arms. The groundhog stood on its hind legs.

The explosion out of the gun was for Jonas to register with his phenomenal ears; he would hear nothing else for days. And years later, at the recollection, he would clamp his palms to his ears and squeeze his eyes shut. I saw the smoke puff, and I followed the bullet, miraculous, with my eyes, tracing its mathematical arc, the slow rise and the slower fall, its wedged entry into the brown shoulder fur of the animal in the center of the garden, just where my mother wanted it, and there, inside the animal, next to the muscled heart, the bullet stopped. It held its warmth there, the way blood does, although its chilling also began when the body first buckled and slipped downward. On its side, the groundhog moved its legs several times, but then its head flattened against the ground, and Jonas and I were the ones who stood up and nodded and waved to my mother. Come here.

There, she said. I did my part.

She wiped the gun with a Kleenex.

With the gun in her arms, she did an about-face and headed up the lawn to the house. Bury it in the field, you two. We'll set up again after lunch.

17

Her voice is not what it was, I said to Jonas.

It's clear to me, he said.

I don't understand one thing she says.

She said to bury the groundhog.

Throw it in the weeds, I said to him. Let it rot.

She said bury it.

Okay. Let a dog dig it up later then.

You're sour, just like she says.

And so I walked off and walked down the middle row of the tobacco field, as I often did, and sat down in the center of the field, under the green roof of the tallest plants. The leaves spread out, tented, over my head, and the heated air felt as smooth as a liquid on my face. I crossed my legs and sat like a foreigner, just fine.

After a while, I stepped to the next row and pulled up my skirt and pulled down my underpants, and sat on my heels and peed in the dirt. Inside my head, in my mother's voice, I heard myself swear: When you are dead and I piss on the ground, then I will say out loud—*Piss on you.*

18 P.S.—A.D., Here you are. Marie de France.

There is a woodcut of Marie de France, on a boat on the Channel. She is dressed in a long gown and standing at the front of the boat, looking out into the waves, which pass by sideways, rolling back, uncovering peculiar fishes and small but monstrous sea creatures—scaled children with limbless bodies, brilliant starfish with long, thin floating hair, like girls'. She is listening to their voices, all across the Channel. They trail her. She notes down their songs, but the sense is distorted, and Marie de France's scribblings read as nonsense. She turns over the tablet—we see the cryptic notations, upside down, backwards—and on the other side, where we cannot see, she writes the songs she has heard all her life, the ordinary Breton lays. She looks at the sea creatures with her half smile, though, and says, All right, you sing that, while I write down *this*. And her ear is cocked towards the sailors behind her, there they are, strumming away again, ignoring the heavy seas, and it's the familiar tune: lovers and lost love. Les Quatre Dols. Four lovers vie for the love of a maiden. Three of them die in this quest. The surviving lover wins not the body of the beloved, not at all. He lives in his kingdom and he lives with his knowledge of love. That's what he wins. It's a sad, sad story. And Marie de France takes this lover's part—she says, I am partial. I can decide the title. Chaitivel, his is the suit most sorrowful. The surviving lover, Chaitivel, there's the story. She writes down his name on the tablet.

Remember, Marie de France has been at court. She sails between one court and another. She knows that love is illicit, always and anywhere. It goes against everything everyone claims they want, everything everyone claims they have, everything there is. It's the ground that gives; it's water under the boat.

Have you found a French book yet, Andrea Doria? Here's her account to the king. You can pick out a few words.

> Ki Deus ad duné escïence
> E de parler bon' eloquence
> Ne s'en deit taisir ne celer,
> Ainz se deit volunters mustrer.

She won't be quiet. *L'amour*, not *les amoureux*, is the story, Marie de France wrote that down in a letter to the king. God is not love, no. The lovers are not. But the story is. Here are the lovers, she says, here are the deaths of lovers, so what? That's finished. What have you got left? What of your wars, your grand barricades, your turrets, your children, your wooded land? Listen to this. Do you want the truth or don't you? Do you want me to write down these songs or don't you?

19

Johnny Smoke and Marlene were our guests. They'd called up the night before and asked to stop by. My mother arranged the chairs in the living room several times, not completely satisfied, until Aunt Sarah brought in two folding chairs and convinced her that everyone could be seated, comfortably, close enough to hear, but not too close, not crowded.

This is fine, Aunt Sarah told her. Count again. If we want, we can all be here. Do you think Jonas will want to be here?

If he's in the house, we'll have him here. We'll all be here.

My mother gave thought to the placement of guests, to an arrangement that kept the most interested parties farthest apart, for a calculated balance of personalities, force opposite force. She alternated, when possible, male and female. Given any collection of people, my mother believed an ideal arrangement could be achieved; it was a skill, a craft, like arranging flowers, so that each contributed to the whole, for a nice effect.

Put Andy on the one folding chair. Sarah, you will be there, by the door. What do you think?

Johnny and Marlene, will you put them together on the sofa?

Of course, said my mother. You'll be there by the door. Is that all right?

That's fine, Aunt Sarah said. I'll be up and down for coffee. You just keep yourself quiet in your chair and I'll do the coffee.

You don't mind being in the door?

I told you, that's fine. I'll be near the kitchen. I don't think it's me that Johnny and Marlene want to talk to. You're the one they know. It's you they're visiting.

Well, when they visit my house, they visit us all, that's how it is. I'm not the only one here. A friend of mine is a friend of yours, Sarah. Will you be comfortable there by the door?

Yes. Just fine.

No one will squeeze in and out past you, I'll see to that. I want you to feel very comfortable. No one should feel left out or pushed in a corner. That's what we want to avoid. It's a small room, but we can have guests and we can arrange things. I told Marlene it's a small house but never mind, she is welcome if she can put up with being a bit cramped in the living room. Do you think she'll be cramped?

It's fine.

What about Johnny Smoke?

What about him?

Will he be comfortable there on the sofa? my mother asked.

Of course. He'll have to be, Aunt Sarah said. If he sits with Marlene, they'll have to be there. Nothing else holds two people. If you want them together.

My mother set my folding chair in the space between her recliner and my father's chair in the corner of the room. How is this, Andy? she said. Try it out.

I sat in the chair, and that's where I was through the visit with Marlene and Johnny Smoke. Marlene had dressed up. She wore dark slacks and black heels with open toes. Her blouse was a silky red one, and her red hair, which looked orange now, curled in long ringlets at the side of her face. When she talked she pushed her shoulders back against the sofa and lifted her chin up.

Jonas sat on the other folding chair, near Aunt Sarah. When he shifted his legs, the metal seat creaked.

Through the summer, Jonas's hair bleached out blond, almost as light as my mother's, and from where I sat in the living room that night, his hair and the top of his ear rose up above my mother's head. If I glanced at my mother, what I saw was a woman with half-curled, half-straight hair, a woman with one ear on the side of her head, one coming out the top. She might have had one or two extra legs, if I'd wanted to look.

20

Even out in the field, with the sunlight flat on the top of my head like a hand, I can tell how they arrange themselves inside the barn on the empty tobacco wagon, the three of them, Jonas, Aunt Sarah, and my father. The sun angles in through the open doors, a yellow parallelogram in the air, light and dust like a cotton cloth, a patch that is so bright everything else in the barn holds as black; and because the light keeps coming in and hanging there, nobody's eyes adjust. The three sit in the dark interior, my father on the plank in the middle of the wagon, with his feet hanging free over the edge. He plays a harmonica. Without moving his body, he puffs in and out. Jonas either swings from the iron bar at the back of the wagon or stretches out on the plank, flat on his back, with his arms extended over his head, just flattening himself out on the board. Aunt Sarah leans against the iron wheel of the wagon and shuts her eyes, listening.

Their faces are lined with dust on the cheeks, and Jonas's hands are coated with tar. He doesn't wear gloves. He won't touch his face with his hands, but he'll wipe his forehead with the uppermost part of his arm, and the white shirt sleeve is brown and damp. Aunt Sarah's and my father's gloves lie in the shape of whole hands on the plank of the wagon, the cotton stiffened with tobacco gum.

In the heat, my mother has gone back into the house.

I hear the harmonica music, the lung work of it, in and

out. The barn might as well be breathing. And then the harmonica gasps, like a woman caught in a room she hadn't known was there, when the lights flick out and the doors lock shut, and there she is. She tries to keep something like liveliness in her voice, but the doors have shut and the torments and joys of the world, all of its colors, have already clicked off, far into the past, and cut themselves off.

I should run to the barn and rescue whoever is in there. But the doors are wide open; they're huge doors. I can see the shape of the sunlight slanting inside. Anyway, if they are held there, my mother, where she is, is farther away. From the house, she would have to walk to the barn, and through the dark of it, and then out the big doors into the field.

The harmonica sounds go crazy. Aunt Sarah laughs along.

When I shake my mother in her chair, she opens her eyes and says, Andy, what is it? She slurs her words, What's the matter?

21

Marlene said, Calm down, prepare yourself—for whatever! Life isn't H_2O in a glass. She kicked at the dirt, digging her feet in her own footprints, and then she picked up a lath and fitted the spear. She said, See, I am the swizzle stick. The air in the cream. The fizz. I'm Carmen Dioxide! she said.

And to confirm, she stripped a tobacco leaf from the stalk she was spearing and clamped its thick stem in her teeth.

Andrea Doria, my cigarette girl! she sang to me, off key, and she flapped the big leaf around me like a scarf. She stamped her feet in the dust to stir up a cloud on each side of me. I see a *soldier* in your future! Or, oh—a conscientious objector! Oh, which will she choose? Marlene addressed the tobacco field, the long uncut rows of stalks, standing ahead. Which will she choose—soldier or medic? Will it be the one who'll break her heart, or the one who'll sew it up!

There aren't any soldiers around here, I said.

But you won't *be* around here. The cigarette factory! Don't you know where farm girls go? Read some history, Andrea Doria.

She finished spearing a lath of five stalks. With some difficulty, she shook it out, straightening the leaves.

You'd do the best thing, for all concerned, wouldn't you? she said.

Probably.

I knew it. The difference between you and me, she said, and she meant the difference between Mennonites and her, is that *you* try to keep an eye on the planet, while I, like the trilobite, watch my step. Here, and here.

What's a trilobite?

Andrea Doria, it's a fossil. Read your geology. It's etched in stone. There it is. There it was. It eked out a living and did what it did. If creatures don't try to change the world, they've done their duty. I've got my niche, now, for the moment. Until I'm ready to move on, and that, as a matter of fact, won't be too far in the future. I've already found my ticket.

I bet it's a man, I said.

Mennonites don't bet. Watch yourself.

I know it's a man.

Sure you do. And why couldn't it be a fat billfold I found on a path?

But it wasn't, was it?

She picked up a little tobacco plant with a thin stem, and she concentrated on it, centering it on the spear. With both hands, she pressed the stalk, wobbled it, until it was speared through and strung on the lath.

At thirteen, I was strong, and growing stronger. Bending down to a plant and up with the stalk in one hand, then down again, and up—for me, it was an easy exercise. My back finally felt like a part of me, with muscles on either side of my backbone, good slopes for the sun to reach. Marlene sweated more than I did, but probably from the exertion of talk. She took advantage of our time in the fields to make sure I wasn't sheltered from the facts of human life. What can a pacifist *do?* she said. Well, all right, there is *strength* in truth, she said, as righteously as she was able, mocking me. Look at the muscle in your arm, Andrea Doria!

I'm tired, I lied. Let's take a break.

All right, she said. That's a good idea. Nothing wrong with that.

We walked to the upper end of the field, to the locust trees in the hedgerow, for a taste of vinegar punch in a cooler by a rock.

Without a wind blowing, even the shade was full of heat, weighted down. Marlene sat on the rock and, leaning over, reached into the edge of the field and dug up two big handfuls of dirt, very dry. She wore cut-off denim shorts and a loose black T-shirt. Her legs were stalky legs, ones she didn't think to cross.

Look, relax! she said. And as if the dirt in her hands were

a lotion or powder, she dumped it onto her knees, and she rubbed it up and down her legs, dusting them.

I stood in the shade, a girl in Mennonite dress. My mother slept in her chair in the house. Everywhere, everything continued.

I didn't know which one of us to pity—I couldn't decide. So, I thought, pity none.

The phrase was all I had, and when we went back to work, I used the words when I used the spear, saying them as I brought the tobacco stalks up, and as I brought them down. Pity none. Pity none. All afternoon, the tobacco stalks—how many withering ones?—split on the spearhead, and I strung them up and lay them down.

22   My mother walked out the door in her red swimsuit, and Jonas and I waited in the yard. We'd filled the blue plastic pool with water, and we'd set a wooden crate at the edge of the pool, as a step.

Here I am, my mother said.

She held out her arms for us to hold, and we helped her up the step and into the pool my father had bought, a large wading pool with a metal edge and a plastic liner. When she stepped in, the metal rim of the pool wobbled and rolled, a flimsy thunder.

My mother stood in the water, to get her footing, and then she bent her knees and sat down. The water came up to her neck. With Jonas on one side and me on the other, we supported my mother's arms while she stretched out and floated her legs.

I'm not so pale, my mother said. She held one leg out of the water and pointed the toes upward.

This has helped a lot, Jonas said.

My mother kicked her feet, up and down and side to side, sending out waves that swept to the edges and splashed up.

Have you tried this? my mother asked. It's warm already.

Not yet, Jonas said. He scooped a handful of water from the pool.

Well, there's nothing like it, my mother said.

She shut her eyes, and I felt her shoulder settle against my arm.

Jonas stirred his hand through the water like a mixer. A whirlpool! he said.

That's nice, my mother said. That's very nice. Andy, churn up the water, she said.

I pushed my fist through the water, a wooden spoon in a kettle, around and around.

Her eyes still shut, my mother breathed out smoothly. Her knees floated to the surface. Her arms stretched out.

23   P.S.—A.D., Today, at Cancale, at low tide, I walked out on the mud flats through the fog. You know I do not neglect your mother or forget her. I thought I would walk there and think about her. But wind pushed into the fog, and nothing remained solid or still—not the oyster beds, not the

men and women out there sorting the catch, and even the sounds moved along unattached, voices saying *here, not there, now, that one, maintenant, celui-là, maintenant.* I came back and finished this work.

Here, read the Prologue to your mother. Tell her it's Marie de France's case, for the court. She wrote at her desk, looking backwards and looking forwards. She knew the parchment would crumble. And her king.

You know that, too, Andrea Doria.

Remember. Read to your mother. It doesn't matter if she doesn't listen.

Those whom God has given knowledge and full eloquence of speech, they must not be silent and secretive, but instead they must willingly reveal themselves. When something of goodness is heard by several, then it blossoms; and when it is praised, even by a few, then it opens its flowers.

It was a custom of the ancients, so claims Priscianus, to speak somewhat obscurely in their books, so that those who came afterwards would interpret the words according to their own sense, and thereby augment the meaning. The philosopher knew that the more time which passes by, the more careful of mind we become and the better able we are to avoid the writer's errors, and so make our own way. Those who would defend themselves against vice must study, and pay heed, and undertake grievous labor; thereby they may avoid transgression and spare themselves great anguish.

Which is why I began to think of composing a pleasant story, translating it from Latin into the Romance tongue. But this would not have meant much to me: so many others had already undertaken it.

Then I thought of the lays I had heard sung. I knew very well, I didn't doubt, that the ones who first made them up and who afterwards sang them forth, had drawn upon other stories they had heard and committed to memory. Several of the songs I heard, I could not neglect or forget. I have put these in verse and made a poem of them, often staying up into the night over them.

In your honor, noble king, who are so worthy and courtly, to whom all joy bows down and in whose heart is rooted all that is fine, I undertook to assemble these lays, to set them in verse and tell them, again. In my heart I conceived and spoke them, Sire, to present them to you. If you are happy to receive them, it would give me great joy, and I would take lasting pleasure. Do not think I am presumptuous if I am so bold in your presence. Now, hear the beginning!

24 Such a small place, a row of Formica tables, edged with chrome, a counter and blue spinning seats, all of the surfaces slick enough to shear off bits of light and send them away in streaks, trailing dust. The walls shimmered. On the tabletop, my father tapped his fingers, one after the other, little finger to index finger, *ta-ta-ta-ta*, so fast the sound blurred to a simple *thrummmm, thrummmm*.

A tenor sang an aria on the radio, and it was a treat for Jonas and me, drawing soda water and foam up through a plastic straw. My father sat with his hat in his lap and sipped on a soda, too.

One of the treasurers at church, my father had driven to the bus station, to pay for a charter, and the Mennonite man at the rental desk said to him, So, they're at it again. I don't know, is a war the same as a flood? Is a march the same as work?

With a slender gold pen between his fingers, the man filled out papers for my father. What does the marching do? the man asked. When they go in afterwards and fix things up, *that* I can take. But marching, that's not help.

It's hard to know, my father said.

He signed the check and walked us across the street to the Blue Ball Diner.

Jonas sat with his chin in his hands and listened to my father's fingers strumming.

I watched my father's eyes looking out the window and down the street, where the road fell away towards a stream. A bridge crossed the stream, out of sight, in a hollow, and then the road rose to the east, came back into view, and turned sharply, out of town. I followed my father's eyes, but how could I see what he saw? The solid line in the pavement? The sycamores? Or, at the far turn of the road, almost a mile away, did he see that dark scrap moving? Somebody crossing the road. Maybe a man, maybe a woman. It was a shape with limbs, upright and walking. That far away, with the intervening trees, the form appeared, then disappeared. Somebody's getting the mail.

My mother did not travel. My feet only take me so far, she said.

A red car passed on the road, and my father stopped drumming his fingers and looked around inside. His eyes followed the countertop along to the soda fountain and then upward to the radio. He put his hands in his lap.

What do you make of the singer? he said to me. He smiled, his lips pressed together under his mustache. From his pocket he pulled out change for a tip.

I listened a moment. He's good, I said.

Well, I'll tell you, my father said, he's not looking on the bright side.

Which bright side? I asked.

It's Italian! Jonas said. We don't know what the trouble is!

No, we don't know, my father said. But it shouldn't sound like the end of the world, should it?

My father rapped his knuckles on a watery square of sun on the table. He stood, and he dropped three dimes there, out of the palm of his hand.

25 It was Marlene's idea: a moonlight look at the lake, it would do my mother good. She needs an outing, Marlene said.

Need has nothing to do with it, I said, but Marlene said she wouldn't argue. It's a good idea, I'll work it out, she said. You help your mother now—be a good girl.

I told her, I don't know what else to be.

My mother stood on the lake shore while Johnny Smoke unlocked the boat shed.

My mother turned around and waved at me. Her long navy-blue dress, a lightweight summer one, moved when she stepped and called attention to her feet, to her ankles. She wore black cotton stockings and flat black shoes. With her feet so apparent, my mother looked sturdy, somehow attached to the sand. And with her ankles showing too, she looked more solid than Johnny Smoke, whose shoe tips peeked out from long pants, discreetly, as he pulled the rowboat from the shed.

Johnny Smoke held the boat while my mother stepped in, and he waited for me, holding the rope, kicking a little sand around his shoes. His jacket glowed, luminescent, in the weak light around the shed.

I'll wait here, I told him. You go ahead.

We'll just row around a little, then, he said. We won't be long.

I helped push them off, and then I sat on the dock and listened. There was some noise from the prison, but at such a distance, it rolled away and upwards, like the noise of a movie outside the theater, or like the noise of heavy machinery behind a hill, at a secluded site.

Where I was, there was only a boat on water. My mother rocking.

26 The violence of the lake, which was a violence of origins and dredgings and the machining of twenty-four acres, re-formed itself into the contours and surfaces of a three-fingered hand. Off balance, the new lake lay on the ground, its palm pressing and pushing.

I could see only three or four lights: the flare of Johnny Smoke's jacket; the slur of the boat's wake, catching up whiteness from somewhere, scattering it; and through the net of the woods, one bright bulb. It could have been the light at our house. But I'd never been at the lake at night; I hadn't studied the angles or measured where the familiars should appear.

The sky was blurred, roughed up and smeared. But the longer I sat, the more trees appeared, an edge to the lake, a stand for the fluid night sky. I could see one thing, and then I could see another.

In the past—how long ago?—when I was with my mother, the earth spun like a planet, always at hand, the flood and the dry air, both, heaven and hell, balled up and thrown together as far from God as my mother could pitch them. And we caught it all up and played. It was more than a child's game. Nobody rooted for anybody. Nobody joined a team. God can take sides if he wants, my mother had said disdainfully, but we ignore that. We play along. All we want, remember, is the *field*. When somebody wins or loses and goes home, then we sit down here and stretch out our legs and that's that.

On the dock, I stretched out my legs. The boards were still warm from the sun, the long September day, and I lay back, as if it were somehow the middle of day, and I shut my eyes. Waves from the rowboat, rolling in, hit the posts underneath with a slap, then splayed out and hushed and drew themselves back.

Offshore, I could make out the boat, a gray little dish, the silver cut of the oar. As I watched, the boat began moving slowly, in a widening circle, a spiral opening outward.

My mother was rowing. Her good arm was pulling well, the other lagging, and if she was aiming towards shore, as she must have been, there was no way for her to aim.

The night smelled of the water, and of tobacco, the aroma carried through the woods, out of the slats of the tobacco shed, and across two fields, between the trunks of all the trees, and into the moist air over the lake, where the scent blended with the smells of the damp: leaf mold, algae, the cleansed metallic smell of the white sand, a mildew and boat smell.

My mother rowed in larger and larger circles, more askew, until she passed close enough to shore for me to hear Johnny Smoke say, Let me angle in, do you see Andrea Doria?

I waved then, and I saw Johnny Smoke take the oars and bring the boat around, straight for me.

Everything quiet? he asked.

I haven't heard anything for a while.

Well, good. We had a nice row-around, he said. I'd better get back now. Back there it's business.

Johnny Smoke helped my mother out of the boat. She landed lightly on the boards and tapped her feet, flat-footed, on the dock.

That was very nice, she said. She checked her footing again and reached for my hand. We can walk back, she said.

All right, go ahead, Johnny Smoke said. Watch your step.

My mother pulled at my hand and held it against her waist. We walked the gravel path this way, like children, me waving my other arm ahead, to catch the small branches in the way or the spiderwebs, and we followed the path markers, painted a glossy white, the diving figure carved in the wood, coolly appearing just when the path took a turn with the wall. Out of the scrubland, the path aimed towards the main gate, where they waved us through. And then we were in our own fields.

Such a nice boat ride, my mother said. Did you see me rowing?

I watched the whole time.

You should have come along, my mother said. Don't worry about the water. You're too much afraid of things. You hang back. That won't get you very far, she said. Make some friends at school, why don't you? Try out for cheerleading.

Cheerleading! What are you talking about, a Mennonite cheerleader!

Well, you could try out, and meet some people. You need something to talk about if you're going to make friends.

I can talk. I have friends.

You know what I mean.

The night air was warm, with a dampness hanging low over the fields. The air of the lake, the air of the wall and the woods, held to us, trailing like cloth. The tobacco fields were in stubble, not yet fall-plowed, and the rows between were littered with dry tobacco leaves, remnants from cutting. They were brittle and dusty. When we stepped on the leaves, they crushed, rattling like paper, or paper ash, disintegrating at the touch. And so it was a noisy, soft walk home, every step pressing a leaf into dust; and the scent of tobacco rose into my mother's skirts.

My mother sighed. She still held my hand, and then she shut her eyes, trusting me to walk her through the stubble.

What do you see when you shut your eyes? I asked her.

Nothing, she said, and she opened her eyes. I see what I see with my eyes open.

27 At the house, my father said to me, Andrea Doria, how about coffee?

He poured a juice glass of brandy for my mother. Her bottle

in the cupboard, a tonic, was the bottle with a tall, narrow neck that a person could grab onto easily and pull out and tip over.

I said, Yes, coffee sounds good.

My father lifted the steel percolator and set a cup on a saucer and placed a spoon on the table for me.

If someone had offered me a cigarette and struck a match, I'd have said, Yes. When a lover would ask someday, Andrea Doria, can you unhook that shirt? I knew I could do it.

I put my fingers over the cup, into the steam. I accepted the coffee the way a person accepts anything offered, the first time, with the heady pleasure of being gathered up, taken aboard, and with another pleasure as well, the sweet-tasting churn of defiance as the heart writes out on its walls: this won't corrupt me either.

28

P.S.—A.D., This dream: the penitentiary walls were in sharp focus, with white mortar outlined around every block; but the noise, the noise of the dream, had no definition at all. It rolled through the air, a machine noise, vocal, raucous, calamitous, the sound of collapse. And the walls did fall down. Very precisely. They cracked along mortar lines, and the cracks widened and blue sky came through. Then the walls flattened out, shapes on the ground. A very slight dust rose out of the rubble, but the noise, an excess, surrounded the ruins and crescendoed. There wasn't anything else.

You and your mother were watching, too. That's the point,

Andrea Doria. The point is, there's nothing to gain, not on the inside. The point is, stay out. That's what a Mennonite wants, no insurance, nothing guaranteed. Even a lapsed Mennonite, and here I am. No warranties, no legal papers. Think what living at court does to a woman, and to the men. Everything turns on real estate. You buy to sell; you buy to build to sell. Romance is set up, opposite commerce, and see what you have. Courtly love.

My little one, I don't know who I'm writing to.

Why don't you, once in a while, read your mother these dreams? Think of it, Andrea Doria. What harm could it do?

29 My mother watches a game show instead of the news. She laughs with Aunt Sarah and tells her, or tells me, See, you see, people can have a good time when they want to.

I sit at the dining room table and do my homework, and my mother says, for my benefit, Laughing never hurt the face. She reaches over towards Aunt Sarah's chair, touches the arm of it, and laughs again with her.

Aunt Sarah's face is set with a permanent pattern of lines that trace her laughter—lines span out from the corners of the eyes and parentheses pull into the cheeks, either side of her mouth. She holds her face in a smile, long after the smile is finished. My mother has adopted Aunt Sarah's rules, having forgotten her own, and now her face, too, smiles through the commercials and smiles whenever a face appears in the room or on the television.

Lighten up, my mother says, in a tone I hardly recognize. She picks up phrases from TV and uses them on me.

Oh, she's busy, Aunt Sarah says. Are we bothering you, Andrea?

I have to write about somebody I don't understand. Two pages. The assignment says: Consider writing about a relative.

You don't understand me, do you, Andy? my mother says. Nobody understands us, she says, and she pats Aunt Sarah's chair again, and they laugh.

I'm doing Daddy, I say.

Oh, good, my mother says. Read it to me when you're finished. Maybe I'll learn a thing or two.

Don't you understand him?

After fifteen years, Aunt Sarah says, she better understand him. That's what marriage is for.

Of course I understand him. We know each other backwards and forwards, my mother says. We've always understood each other. I just want to hear what *you* think. I don't know why you'd think you don't understand him.

He doesn't complain about much.

Nobody tells you their problems, my mother says, unless you ask. Ask people questions, talk to them. Or pretty soon you won't understand anybody.

The assignment would be easier, then, wouldn't it? I say.

Oh, pooh, Aunt Sarah says. She laughs her laugh. You're being snooty, Andrea. Just write your paper. We'll be quiet over here.

Shh, my mother says, and laughs with Aunt Sarah, and squints her eyes. Hush your mouth.

30 After Halloween, when the tobacco leaves were cured from green to amber to flat brown, we worked in the evenings in the shed, taking the laths down from the rafters and hanging them in the cellar of the shed, where we watered the stalks with a watering can. Down there, the leaves moistened, and in a few days we could touch them and bend them, and strip them from the stalk.

Taking down was silent work, because of the cold, and because we needed to listen for the sound of the rattling stalks coming downward through the dark, from the tiers above. A swinging trouble-light made more shadow than light, with the shed's posts and machinery blocking the bulb no matter where it hung.

Overhead, my father worked, sometimes two stories up. I stood on the floor of the shed, catching the descending laths, unhooking them from the rope, and handing them on through a trapdoor in the floor to Jonas, in the cellar, who hung the laths on frames along the stone foundation.

There were times when, above me, I could see my father's breath, shreds of it, floating down. My own breath drifted away like a winter shrub, a snowy thing rolling through the dark.

I thought about writing the scene to Ruth as a dream. But she would have noticed my mother's absence, and looked for her, inside and out.

And the truth is, my mother did sometimes wander out on

the nights we worked in the barn. She walked along the edges of the fields until Aunt Sarah called out the back door, and then my mother returned. I could hear the back door open and close, the brief catches of Aunt Sarah's swaying voice, up and down, and my mother's laughing—short, disconnected sounds rising and then starting over and rising again.

Working in the shed, that's what I saw of my mother, the dark shape of her, going in the door, with the boxed-up yellow light of the house wrapping around her. Aunt Sarah put her to bed.

We worked slowly, in the cold of the shed. Each lath swung down from my father, and I caught the end of it in one hand, unhooked the rope with the other hand, and then the stalks were mine, to lift away from the floor and to carry to the trapdoor, not letting the leaves brush my coat. The leaves were drier than any skin, fragile as anything pressed between the pages of a book.

I tipped the lath down the open trapdoor to Jonas, past the top of his head, his red knit cap, and into his outstretched hands. When he took a lath from me, I breathed out a foggy puff of air and watched it sail away, and then I straightened up and walked back to the place where I could hear the next lath of tobacco coming down. There was a bright flash of leaf as the light caught its descent.

No tourists here, my father called down.

No Skryzinski, Jonas called back, his voice rising up and the sounds rising up, too, up a scale.

He wasn't a tourist, I said. I bet you don't remember him.

Sure I do. He took notes.

He's dead, I said.

Well, Jonas said, he's not here.

Nobody's here, my father said.

When they shut themselves up this way, with this talk, that's when I let the walls of the barn fall away, fold out and fall to the ground, very quietly. A deliberate work. The frame of the barn, the tiers where my father walked, held secure, and he went on about his business, hardly aware of the shift in the darkness, from the wavering interior dark to the flowing night sky, just as black, just as cold, but ongoing, and full of the breathing of neighbors and prisoners and tourists, and open to birds, bats, the gunsights of missiles, the eyes of the blind, and anyone waking or sleeping. Ruth was nearby. My mother could stroll right in.

But God, who preferred the inside of the inside, and who liked to keep everything under wraps, stayed put, in his hole. Though my mother had come to deny it, one thing I knew I could count on: God never moved a muscle.

31 My father collects the flimsy tobacco stalks we have stripped. The leafless stalks are mottled green and brown, the pith already gone to mush. In the stripping room, he presses the stalks into bales and ties the bales with twine. He lifts each one, light as a pillow, under his arm, and takes it outside to the stack that is building up by the south wall of the shed. In the spring, we'll heap the stalks in the manure spreader and drive around, big circles in the fields, letting the stalks fly. The stems even now are cushiony through the middle, and by April they will have turned black and will rot back into the soil, in soft strips.

While my father is outside, Jonas picks up a floppy stalk that has fallen out of the bale and leans on it, for a walking stick. He limps around the stripping room, playing the little old man, with the squashy cane.

The fire in the heater glows through a crack in the iron door, and Jonas stumbles towards the fire, cackling in an old man's voice: I'll grind your bones to bake my bread.

He's a tall boy, and he leans down on the stalk and buckles over; he folds himself almost in half to be little.

He throws another stalk to me and both of us dance like cripples. Jonas cackles some more. He circles the potbellied stove and ducks under the stovepipe that cuts through the wall.

My father opens the stripping room door, and out of the flat rectangle of dark, he steps into the room. He looks very large and three-dimensional, a shape puffed up with its life, and Jonas stops in mid-step for a minute. He straightens up and then dips down again, pressing the stalk against the floor.

My father says, I'll get us some more to strip.

He goes through a door in the wall behind Jonas, into the adjacent tobacco cellar. Jonas and I lift ourselves onto the sizing table and lean our heads back so that even our hair falls into the brown tobacco dust. My feet, near the fire, are warm, and my head, at the pane of the window, takes the chill from the glass.

Outside, beyond the reach of the room's light, upside down, I can make out the shape of my mother's feet, walking by. She's wearing her summer stockings, the light ones, and dark shoes. Her dress must be dark, too, because it reflects no light, and she passes like a drawing of someone walking, the legs apparent.

I sit up. Usually my mother waves. But now, when she does not, I follow her arm, a deeper shadow, until I see her hand moving at her side, up and down as she walks.

She's holding the barrel of her gun.

She walks like a person with a cane, leaning on the gun. Light gleams off the metal, a long narrow stripe flickering ahead of her, and then swinging back.

Wait here, I say to Jonas.

Outside, I give my eyes time to adjust. My mother does not walk very fast, and I won't have trouble finding her. The night shifts, gradually, from a flat blackboard, erased, to receding, flimsy gray vapors, and then those disappear. The fields open up ahead to the woods. Finally, the air is simply black, clear as water.

My mother is in the middle of the stubble field, moving away. She sails along. Her dress slaps, cloth against cloth, I can hear that, and setting my head down, pulling my chin against my chest, I lean forward and walk as fast as I can to catch up with her. The ground is frosted, just on the surface, and it cracks and breaks where I step. I'm leaving tracks. The air is cold, and I stick my hands in the pockets of my dress, and before long, I'm running, without my arms, awkward and off balance, each step, but I'm running, and my mother is slowing.

At the edge of the tobacco field, she stops and leans on the gun.

You better come back, I call.

Oh! she says. And she sinks, sitting, onto the ground. So it's you, she says. What's the matter?

You don't need a gun at night.

What? I'm going on the boat.

You don't need a gun in the boat.

A gun? My mother looks at the gun on the ground, under her hand.

She shakes her head, side to side, and laughs several puffing laughs. My mistake, she says. Look at that.

She shakes her head some more, and then she picks up the gun with one hand and gives it to me. Her arm is steady. I take the stock, behind the thumbnail curve of the trigger.

You can have it, she says.

I help my mother up, and she stands for a moment, looking all around. She pulls a thick strand of hair down along the side of her face, and she twists the hair around her finger and lets it fall, a long coil in front of her ear. She takes the tip of the curl and sticks it in her mouth.

Her face is her new, accommodating face, and I feel better in the darkness when she turns and looks away from me, when I see only the back of her head, her hair pulled unevenly into the prayer cap. Her shoulders slope under the heavy coat, lopsided as if she had pulled it across her back, something too large. The darkness of the coat washes completely into the darkness of the air, and she appears to be a construction for the transportation of night—a homemade device that carts a wedge across the field. Her legs, in the wrong stockings, glow very white. Her feet, sunk in black shoes, disappear into the ground. When she walks away from me, her legs carry her. Her hair points in all directions.

32

She walked farther into the field, and not far away, she fell.

Where she fell, there was no water. Nothing to buoy her. And she folded downward and broke hard to the side. The closest body of water was the lake, and what could it hold and keep? The Susquehanna, beyond the hill, wide and ranging, took everything with it, as part of itself. And the oceans, all of the planet's oceans, were too far away now to reach.

In the middle of the field, I aimed the gun straight up and fired it.

I yelled towards the barn, Come here!

When I dropped the gun and ran towards my mother, the air swept around me and over my head; it parted slowly—I could feel its parting and its reconvergence, behind my back.

I thought for a moment the gunshot had punctured the sky, our own roof. And water had poured in, and the blackness had ripped apart, tearing south to north, and water had fallen through air, and the air had swept with water until my mother, a stalk, a tree, had been lifted from where she was. With her coat slipped away and her shoes kicked off, she would have already opened her eyes, brought her hands together, and dived.

Four

1 After so many years, who are the ones I could approach and ask, Did you ever know?

Have you forgotten?

My daughter will hear what there is to hear.

You have your grandmother's daylight eyes, I'll start with that. Look in the mirror, I'll say. God did not dream up such eyes.

I'll mention the one whose eyes contain yellow, irregular shards in the iris; and she will say, Who is that? I don't know what I'll say. I'll fill in some details. I'll tell her about tobacco, a velvet plant, unwieldy. I'll give her my mother's binoculars.

If she asks for more facts, I'll tell what I know. I know this. I'll say, sweet pie, forget the facts. Remember, your grandmother wasn't herself. Remember that.

But she died before I was born, she'll say.

You're right. She did.

I bet she's in Heaven, my daughter will say.

And I will say, No.

You're lying, she'll say.

I'll tell her, No, no, I'm not. Your grandmother swims in Hell, I know this. Her face is pure bone now—look—turning easily side to side, sluicing the flames, each cheek resting in fire briefly, and there—look—there are the working bones of her legs and her feet, her arms and her hands, incorruptible.

A NOTE ABOUT THE AUTHOR

Janet Kauffman's collection of short stories, *Places in the World a Woman Could Walk*,
was honored by receipt of the Richard and Hinda Rosenthal Foundation award.
For her poetry, she received a grant from the National Endowment for the Arts.
Ms. Kauffman lives in Michigan, where she farms and also teaches.

A NOTE ON THE TYPE

The text of this book was set in a computer version of Garamond, a modern rendering
of the type first cut in the sixteenth century by Claude Garamond (1510–1561).
Garamond was a pupil of Geoffroy Tory and is believed to have based his letters on the
Venetian models, although he introduced a number of important differences.
It is to him we owe the letter which we know as old style. He gave to his letters
a certain elegance and a feeling of movement which won for himself
an immediate reputation and the patronage of King Francis I of France.

Composed by Crane Typesetting Service, Inc., Barnstable, Massachusetts
Printed and bound by Fairfield Graphics, Fairfield, Pennsylvania
Typography and binding design by Dorothy Schmiderer